BASEBALL BONUS KID

BASEBALL BONUS KID

BY STEVE GELMAN

Illustrated by
JOHN FLOHERTY, JR.

Doubleday & Company, Inc.
Garden City, New York

F
G

LIBRARY OF CONGRESS CATALOG CARD NUMBER 61–12525
COPYRIGHT © 1961 BY DOUBLEDAY & COMPANY, INC.
ALL RIGHTS RESERVED
PRINTED IN THE UNITED STATES OF AMERICA

PREPARED BY RUTLEDGE BOOKS

contents

chapter 1

HOORAY FOR THE HERO

The earth seemed to tremble beneath Bobby Reynolds' feet each time the big bass drum boomed. Bobby could not believe it was happening to him. He was on his way to spring training camp. In less than five hours he would be joining a big league baseball club. And everybody in Waring, Indiana, it seemed, had come to the airport to wish him luck.

"Hold it there, Bobby! Smile! Big smile!"

The newspaper men were clicking their cameras. Bobby posed but his mind was wandering. It was as though he were acting out a dream.

"Make believe you are swinging a bat. Big swing! Home run!"

The cameras continued to click.

The bass drum boomed again. The high school band, all dressed up in spangled green uniforms, filled the air with ear-splitting music.

The crowd began to sing. "Take me out to the ball game. Take me out with the crowd . . ."

Bobby balanced himself on one foot, then on the other, trying to see through the crowd. He was looking for his mom and dad.

A big red and black sign caught his eye. OUR OWN BABE RUTH.

He smiled. "Imagine," he thought, "comparing me and Babe Ruth. Some people are nuts." He was happy, though. It was nice to be compared with the greatest hitter who ever lived.

A cold wind whipped across the Waring airport, shooting a chill through Bobby's big-boned body. "In a few hours I will be in Florida," he thought, "where it will be nice and warm."

Bobby brushed a lock of blond hair from his forehead. He stretched the full length of his six feet four inches, again looking for his parents in the crowd.

"Hey, Golden Boy," a fellow yelled. "What did you do with your $60,000? Spend it on sodas?"

For a split second Bobby's face flushed with anger. Ten months before, the Cleveland Sox had signed him to a $60,000 contract, and he had been hearing jokes about the money ever since.

The contract is the kind that, in baseball, is called

a bonus, a special reward given to many young players who have been stars on their school teams and who are good enough to be given a chance to play in big league baseball. It is a chance the big leagues take with young players. Some of the young players make it, some do not.

Actually, if Bobby made good, the $60,000 would be paid him over five years. But nobody wanted to believe this. All of the people in Waring seemed to think that Bobby Reynolds had become rich overnight. Even his best friends laughed whenever Bobby said he did not have a fortune in the bank.

Finally, he caught sight of his dad. Paul Reynolds was beaming. His chest was thrown out, his head was held high. His pride was bursting out of him for everybody to see.

"He is even happier than I am," Bobby thought. "He has been dreaming of this ever since I was born. It must have been funny, the nurse walking in and saying, 'Mr. Reynolds, it's a boy,' and Dad rushing out to buy a small baseball bat."

He thought of how his dad must have looked in the hospital waving the bat and boasting, "My boy is going to be a big league ball player. This is to get the idea in his head right from the beginning."

Bobby could not remember ever wanting to be anything but a baseball player. He thought back to when he was seven, sitting on the floor, a baseball cap pushed back on his head, listening to stories about Babe Ruth. "I sure worshiped Ruth," Bobby thought. "I used to jump up and clap every time Dad told about one of the Babe's home runs.

Bobby looked at the red and black sign. OUR OWN BABE RUTH. He saw himself at the age of 10, really playing the part of a big league star. He remembered waving his finger toward centerfield and yelling, "I'm going to hit a home run. Right out there."

He could almost hear the other 10-year-olds screaming, "Show off, show off." He had not cared. He had let the first pitch come over the plate. "Strike one," he had said, holding up a finger. He had let the second pitch fly past him, too. "Strike two," he had said, holding up two fingers and pointing with them to centerfield.

"I must have been a show off," Bobby thought, looking up as an airplane roared toward the clouds.

He remembered taking the next pitch perfectly and belting it high over the centerfielder's head. He had run around the bases, laughing, and then jumped into his dad's arms. "I called my homer and then I hit it," Bobby had yelled. "Just like Babe Ruth in the 1932 World Series."

The grin that spread over his dad's face had made Bobby feel warm. "Like the grin he has right now," Bobby thought, catching sight of him.

The newspaper men crowded in again.

"Who helped you the most, Bobby?"

"Who taught you how to hit?"

Bobby smiled at his dad. Paul Reynolds smiled back. "My dad helped me the most," Bobby said. "He used to play ball with me almost every night."

The newspaper men scribbled on their pads. "Where did you play, in the back yard?"

"No. Down by the school. That big lot next to Waring High School. We would play from five o'clock until about six-thirty, starting as soon as Dad got home from work."

The noise from the crowd almost drowned out the next question.

"Did you always play the outfield?" someone shouted.

"Just about. I fooled around at shortstop once in a while, but Dad didn't like it. He kept telling me I had to learn to play one position if I wanted to make the big leagues."

Bobby had heard all these questions before. He had answered them before. His mind wandered. He thought about the lessons his dad had taught him. Go after a fly ball with the crack of the bat. Scoop up base hits and throw with the same motion. Wait for a good pitch. Take a smooth, level swing. Day in, day out, the same lessons. Then one day, he remembered, there had been a different lesson. It was his birthday. He was 13 years old and his dad had brought him many presents. One of them had looked so funny—a bright blue, hard baseball cap.

"What's that?" Bobby had asked.

"This is a helmet to protect your head," his dad had answered. "I want you to wear it when you bat today. If you get hit in the head by a pitch, the ball will bounce off, and you won't get hurt."

They had gone out to the ball field, then and there, to try out the new cap. "I thought he was mad at me," Bobby said to himself. "Those first two times I was up at bat, he threw the ball right at my head."

The scene was clear in Bobby's memory. There he was, 13-year-old Bobby Reynolds, skinny and scared, standing at the plate in the empty lot. On the pitcher's mound, his dad reared back and fired a fast ball— straight at Bobby's head. The ball bounced off his hard covered cap. He remembered the plop it made.

"Hit the dirt when the ball comes at your head," his dad yelled. "Get down or get hit."

Again a high kick on the mound and another fast ball at Bobby's head. He dropped to the ground. "That's the way. That's the way."

The next pitch crossed the center of the plate. But there was Bobby lying in the dirt. "Perfect strike," his dad laughed. "Get up and hit."

"I learned a lesson that day," Bobby said to himself. "I learned an important lesson: when to duck and when to stand up and swing. I felt good when Dad put his arm around me as we walked home. I felt like a real ball player."

How had his father said it? "Son, I guess I was a little rough, but in the big leagues you will have to know when to protect yourself by falling and when to stand up. If you don't know how to duck, you may get hurt. And if you duck at every close pitch, those big curve balls will strike you out every time."

"Dad should be a hero," Bobby thought. "So should Sage Hawkins. If I'm a hero, they should both be heroes, too. They taught me everything."

Bobby remembered the first time he had met Sage Hawkins. Trying out for baseball at Waring High, though he was only in the ninth grade, standing there listening to Coach Hawkins. Sage Hawkins, the famous big-league player, the coach at Waring for 15 years. And the great moment when practice ended. "You've made the team," Sage had said. "You listen to me and learn, boy, and you can be good. You can have big-league scouts chasing you by the time you're a junior."

"Old Sage sure was right," Bobby thought. "He knew what he was talking about. He taught me how to hit curve balls. I banged them my junior year."

The trees at the edge of the airport shook in the wind. Bobby watched them tremble. "Trees are to hit baseballs over," he thought, smiling. "Like the trees in centerfield at the Waring High stadium. Thought I would never be strong enough to hit the ball over those trees, but I did. Still don't know how I grew so fast, from five-eight to six-two between tenth and eleventh grades. From 160 pounds to 190 pounds. Boy, what a surprise that first game I played as a junior. Caught that curve ball right on the fat part of the bat and put it over the trees. I couldn't believe it. The ball went 400 feet. Got my picture in the paper the next day and everybody started to write stories about me."

He thought about the last high school game he had played, the one against Hastings to decide who was to be the new state champion.

It had been warm and sunny that day. Perfect baseball weather. In the stands, screaming students jumped up and down, cheering for Waring, cheering

for Hastings. For eight innings of the game, the boys and girls from Hastings felt sure they had the game won. Hastings had scored two runs in the first inning and Waring had not been able to score at all.

But Bobby and the Waring ball players had other ideas. "We had to win," Bobby thought.

He could remember everything that happened in the ninth inning. Quick singles by the first two Waring batters and then his slow walk up to the plate. Noise from the stands, people yelling at him to hit the ball and win the game. He remembered squeezing the bat handle. Then the fast ball came over the plate. Bobby swung and connected. The ball sailed over the centerfield trees. A roar from the Waring fans shook the stands. Bobby raced around the bases and stood for a second with both feet on home plate. He had made Waring the state champion.

The home run against Hastings really had been something. Graduation Day came the next week and Bobby had walked up to the stage to get the medal given each year to the student who is best in sports. The whole crowd had leaped to its feet. Everybody. Boys and girls in black caps and gowns. Parents and relatives in suits and fancy dresses. They had leaped to their feet to cheer for him. "The best ball player in the history of Waring High," the principal had said. Imagine that.

But the best news had come the day after gradua-

tion. "All those scouts," Bobby remembered, "coming to the house. Scouts from seven big-league teams. Seven scouts with seven bonus offers."

That had been quite a day. All of them sitting around the dining-room table and Dad and Sage Hawkins reading the names of the players of all seven clubs. His father had said that it was up to Bobby to decide. Then Dad had told him to see where he would have the best chance to make good.

"Gee, that was funny," Bobby thought. "We all decided at once—the Cleveland Sox. All the players in their outfield were over 30. They all had said it at the same time, his father, Sage and Bobby. "All the

Sox outfielders are older. Let's sign with the Sox."

The day he signed the contract flashed through Bobby's mind. It had been the biggest moment of his life. First, the Sox general manager signing the $60,000 contract. Then Bobby signing and turning to hand the pen to his dad. "I was glad I was only 18," Bobby thought. "I was glad Dad had to sign the contract. I don't think I was ever closer to him in my life than when we both held that pen."

That was how he had signed his contract and gone to play baseball in Oakmont, California, for the rest of the summer. It wasn't the major leagues, but Oakmont was owned by the Sox and it was just a step away from the majors. It was rated as a Triple A team and most players felt lucky if they ever got that far. "Playing at Oakmont was like a fairy tale," Bobby thought. The first game had been a night game. "Getting up at bat and looking at all those people and knowing I was almost a big league baseball player. And then looking out at the pitcher, Gino Lorenzo, who had played in the big leagues. And hitting a homer my first time at bat—against a guy who had pitched in the big leagues."

Bobby had played well in Oakmont, better than anyone had hoped for a boy straight from high school. In September he had come back home, not knowing where the Sox would tell him to play the next spring. In the fall and winter he did what the

Sox told him to do. He found a delivery job that helped him keep his legs strong. Then it had happened. A telegram from the Sox telling him to go to Florida for spring training, to try out for the major leagues!

Bobby thought of something else. Oakmont and the big leagues are a long way apart. The big leagues and Oakmont can't compare. The real ball players are in the big leagues. "Knock them dead? I just hope they don't knock me dead!"

The plane was ready for boarding. Everybody was waving goodby. Bobby saw his mother. She was waving a copy of the Waring *Times*. Bobby had read it that morning and knew the sports-page story by heart. It began, SOX COUNTING ON GOLDEN BOY REYNOLDS TO HELP BRING THEM THE LEAGUE PENNANT.

"Nice story," Bobby said to himself, "but I wonder if we all aren't expecting too much."

As Bobby climbed the steps to the plane that would take him to Florida, he turned and waved to the crowd. Trumpets played the Waring school song.

"Good luck, Golden Boy," Sage Hawkins yelled. "Remember all of us when you start hitting those homers."

Inside the plane, Bobby took off his overcoat and stretched out in a seat. "I wonder what the papers will be calling me next week," he thought. "Maybe, by then, the Golden Boy will be the Golden Bust."

chapter 2

HERE COMES GOLDEN BOY

Saint Petersburg, Florida, buzzed with baseball excitement. In less than 24 hours, the Sox would begin spring training. Ball players poured into town. They hopped out of long, sleek cars. They walked quickly down airplane steps. They stepped into the warm sun after overnight train rides from the cold North. They were ready and eager to play ball.

The next day, the baseball field would be full of activity. But now it was almost empty. A gray-haired man who took care of the grounds pulled a hose around, sprinkling the grass with water. Only Manager Yank O'Connor was watching him. Yank was waiting for his four coaches. He had called them to the field for a last-minute meeting.

When the coaches arrived, they tried on their baseball uniforms and spiked shoes. Then Yank led them to a large lecture hall, generally used for team meetings. He stood before an open window, the Florida sun warm on his almost bald head. He talked about the team and he talked about different plays. Finally he talked about the rookies, as the new players are called.

"We have a kid coming up who can be great," Yank said. "You all know about him. He is Bobby Reynolds, the bonus kid. Now I want no one, and I mean no one, to talk about batting with Reynolds. I do not want him to become mixed up with advice. I think he is a good hitter, so don't suggest anything to him unless he asks for it."

Yank waved a hand at his coaches. "You coaches," he said, "are responsible for getting that message to the players. Each player must be told."

The men filed out of the meeting room and clumped down the hall, their baseball spikes digging into the wooden floor. As they reached the outside porch, Yank looked out at the highway. He saw a yellow car with its top down roaring toward town.

"Must be Tenda," Yank thought. "He was due in today. Say, he is one guy I had better speak to myself. If any coach talks to him about Reynolds, Tenda is likely to sock him."

At that very moment Tom Tenda, in his car, was

thinking about Bobby Reynolds. Tom's tough face grew tight. He stepped down hard on the gas. "Wonder if that bonus kid is here yet," Tom thought. "That lucky, show-off, Golden Boy."

Tenda's powerful hands gripped the wheel as he steered the car around a curve. "I worked hard to buy this car," he said to himself. "I played baseball for years before I reached the major leagues. I learned how. By the time I got to the Sox, I had proved myself. I didn't walk out of high school and have somebody hand me $60,000 like that Reynolds kid."

Tenda liked to let off steam. It was better than holding it in. He exploded in the locker room when the Sox announced that they had signed Bobby for $60,000. Tom kicked a locker and threw his uniform on the floor. "What a joke," he bellowed. "A kid gets $60,000 before he hits one big-league home run and look what I get after hitting more than 200."

Tom thought now about walking right up to this bonus kid, Bobby Reynolds, and getting him into a home-run contest. "He can bet his $60,000 bonus on the contest," he thought. "Winner take all."

All Bobby Reynolds knew as he walked off the plane in Saint Petersburg was that the warm sun felt good and the future seemed very exciting. There was nothing that might warn him about Tom Tenda.

"What great weather," Bobby said to the attendant at the counter where he picked up his suitcase.

"It's strange, I was freezing just a few hours ago."

The news dealer scooped up a copy of the *Star*. As he handed it over, his eyes ran the full length of Bobby's six feet four. The bonus kid walked away, wondering if the man knew he was a ball player. Bobby had not grown used to being stared at. He would blush every time someone asked him to sign his name for an autograph.

Outside the airport, Bobby hailed a cab. "Park Towers Hotel," he said. He sat back in the leather seat, glad that the driver had not asked him if he was with the baseball team staying there.

The cab rode easily along the highway. Bobby drank in the sights, staring long and hard at the palm trees. He had always liked them. "If I make it big," he had once told his mother, "I am going to get you and Dad a winter home in California or Florida."

"Park Towers," the driver said, snapping Bobby out of a daydream.

"That was quick," Bobby said, mostly because he thought he should say something.

Bobby fished in his pocket and dug out some money. He peeled off two single bills and handed them to the driver. "Keep the change," Bobby said.

"Not much of that," the driver said. "The fare is a dollar-eighty."

Bobby reached in his pocket for a coin. As he

handed it to the driver, he realized it was a half-dollar, not a quarter. "Darn," he thought. "Now the guy will think I am a jerk for tipping too much."

Bobby picked up his heavy suitcase and carried it with almost no effort into the Park Towers. A boy rushed up, grabbed the suitcase, but could hardly lift it. "Sure wish I was a Superman like you," he said, grinning at Bobby.

Bobby grinned back. Then he looked around the red-carpeted room. He was sure he would see some Sox players. Yes, there were catcher Tom Tenda and shortstop Bill Sunderlin talking in a far corner of the room. There was centerfielder Barry Regan at the hotel desk. Regan had always been one of Bobby's favorite ball players. It was hard to believe now that he was on the same team. It seemed only yesterday that Bobby had sat in front of the television set at home cheering hard for Regan.

Bobby wanted to meet the centerfielder. He wanted to tell him how much he had enjoyed watching him play. "Why not just go over?" he thought. "We're teammates now. Barry Regan and I."

The first few steps were slow. Then Bobby got up his courage. "Barry Regan?" he said. The ball player nodded. "I'm Bobby Reynolds, we are teammates. I have always admired you."

Regan frowned. "So you're the kid who got the $60,000," he said. He looked him over.

"Yes," Bobby answered, a smile on his face.

"You are a centerfielder, aren't you?"

Bobby nodded. Regan frowned again. "That means you are trying out for my job."

"I guess so," said Bobby.

"Right," Regan said. "And we are not teammates until you make this team. Right now you are just a fresh rookie. Because you got a bonus, don't think you are someone special. Don't think you are on this team yet."

Regan turned his back and signed the register. Bobby could not believe it. He stood still for a full minute. What could he say? For that matter, what had he said already? He wanted to tell Regan he was sorry they both were centerfielders. He wanted to explain that it was not his fault. And, for a split second, he wanted to grab his suitcase, turn around and go home.

Instead, Bobby signed the register, too. Then he took the elevator to his floor. He walked in a daze to his room and went inside.

Bobby slammed his suitcase down and flipped the light switch. The dark room became alive with light. "Hey, is it morning already? What's going on here?"

Someone leaped out of one of the long twin beds. He rubbed his eyes and ran a hand through his mussed-up black hair. "Hey, you sharing my room?" he asked. "I'm Tony Luco. I was taking a nap."

Bobby smiled. He shook hands with Tony. "I'm Bobby Reynolds," he said. "Pleased to meet you. I am sorry I woke you up."

"That's okay. I swear, I thought it was morning. This is still afternoon, isn't it?"

Bobby laughed. "Yes, it is. Early afternoon."

Tony waved a hand around the room. "Here it is," he said. "Our home for a month."

Bobby looked around the room. "Not bad," he said. He liked the gray and red design of the carpet. The beds were large and they looked comfortable. A radio was nice to have and a big one rested on the long, double dresser. The small desk near the window would be good enough for writing letters home. Bobby walked to the window and looked out. "Nice

view," he said. "You can see the water from here."

"Sure is a nice view," Tony said. "Nice room, too. Everything is nice in the big leagues. I could get to like this life. I am one rookie who wants to stay in the big leagues."

Bobby grinned. "Here is another," he said, tossing his suitcase on his bed.

"Hey," Tony said. "You see Speed Peters yet?"

"No," Bobby said. "Who is Speed Peters?"

"The man who works for the Sox and gets special stories about the team into the newspapers. He must have called the room a million times already. He said to tell you to meet him downstairs."

"I had better go down right now," Bobby said.

"Okay," said Tony. "Back to sleep for me. Kick me before you put on the lights again. Hey, nice meeting you."

"Nice meeting you," Bobby said. "See you later."

Bobby walked to the elevator, wondering what Speed Peters wanted. He stepped onto the main floor and looked around. "I wonder what Speed Peters looks like," he thought.

"Reynolds! Hey, Reynolds! Wait a second!"

Bobby turned. A short man was waving at him. He was standing near the entrance to the coffee shop, looking tiny next to the ball players he had been talking to. Bobby recognized them. Tom Tenda and Bill Sunderlin. Bobby walked over.

"Speed Peters," the fellow said, offering a limp hand. "The Sox publicity man."

Bobby reached out and shook Speed's hand with a firm grip.

"Easy there, boy," Speed said. "I might want to use those fingers again."

"Sorry," Bobby said.

Speed looked up into Bobby's face. "Where you been, boy?" he said. "Some writers have been waiting in the coffee shop all day to see you."

Without introducing him to the ball players, Speed took Bobby's arm and led the way into the coffee shop. "Just think before you speak," Speed said. "Be careful or some of those writers will trap you. You may say things that will get you into trouble. They want to write some big stories about you, boy."

As Bobby walked away, Tenda kicked the wall, and then pounded his fist into his hand. "Did you see that?" Tenda said. "Did you see that? The kid isn't here ten minutes and the writers are waiting for him. They sit inside and wait for him . . . a rookie who never played a single game in the major leagues and the writers are waiting for him."

"Nobody is waiting for me," Sunderlin said. "Nobody is waiting for you. We have only been in the big leagues for ten years."

Tenda turned and shook his fist. "Oh, brother," he bellowed. "Golden Boy has arrived!"

chapter 3

TIME TO PLAY BALL

In the locker room, everybody was moving, everybody was talking at once, slapping one another on the back, wishing each other luck. Spring training was beginning.

A little man moved in between the big ball players, handing out uniforms. Bobby looked at his uniform and ran his fingers along the letters SOX. He held the shirt against his face.

"I can't believe it," he said to Tony. "Me, with a big-league uniform in my hands. My own big league uniform."

"I can't believe it either," Tony said. "It is great, just great."

The two rookies stood in a corner, alone. No one

spoke with them. No one wished them luck. But Bobby tried not to care. Next year, maybe it would be different. By then, he hoped, he would be one of the gang. Now he would just wait. As soon as practice began, he would show them that he deserved to belong.

The booming voice of Manager Yank O'Connor stopped all the conversation. "Out on the field," he ordered. "Everybody out on the field. Come on, play ball."

Bobby pulled his uniform shirt over his head. He tugged up his pants and laced his spiked shoes. He ran out on the field. He was ready to go.

Exercises came first. O'Connor filled the air with commands. "On your backs! Legs in the air! Let me see those legs move. One-two-three-four. One-two-three-four. Move those legs. Move those legs!"

Bobby moved his legs. He lay on his back and churned at the air. "Like riding a bicycle upside down," he thought.

"One-two-three-four. One-two-three-four. On your feet! Let's run! Everybody run! Come on, Regan. Vacation is over. Around the field. Everybody run!"

Bobby ran. His arms swung easily. His long legs ate up distance. He ran until the sweat poured down his face.

"Let me see you throw those baseballs around!

Everybody throw a baseball around. Play ball! Let's go! Play ball! Vacation is over!"

Bobby pulled his glove out of his back pocket. He played catch with Tony. The ball slapped into their gloves with loud pops. The sun beat down on their heads.

Men taking pictures for the newspapers and movies swarmed over the green grass. They shoved each other out of the way, fighting for good angles. They snapped their cameras as fast as their fingers could move.

"Look this way, Reynolds! Over here! Throw the ball! Catch the ball! Hold it! One more! Smile!"

Bobby looked around. All of the men taking pictures seemed to be surrounding him. "That's funny," he thought. "Why aren't they taking pictures of the stars? Why aren't they around Tenda and Regan?"

All morning, Bobby played ball. "We want to take pictures of the players at bat," the cameramen said. "Would you come over to the batting cage please?"

Tenda and Regan were posing by the batting cage as Bobby approached. When Bobby picked up a bat, the newspaper men ran over to him. "That's all," they said to Tenda and Regan. "Thanks."

Bobby swung his bat. The cameras ground away. "Please move into the sun," a fellow said. "These will be color pictures for a magazine cover."

Regan groaned as he bit off some tobacco. "Maybe

we should go away and hide," he said. "We don't want to get in the way of Golden Boy."

Tenda twisted his huge hands around a practice bat. "I used to get a little attention around here," he said. "But I earned everything I got."

Bobby heard them. "What are they angry about?" he thought. "What am I supposed to do? I am not asking those guys to take my picture."

Finally, the cameramen were finished. Bobby walked into the locker room. He tried to joke about the pictures. "Are you sure this is the Sox spring training camp?" he said. "It seems more like Hollywood to me."

A few of the younger players smiled, but the older ones paid no attention to him. Bobby stripped off his uniform and wrapped a towel around his middle. He walked to the shower room. The cold concrete felt good under his bare feet. He hung his towel on a hook and turned on the water full blast.

The warm water pounded his back. It helped his tired muscles. "Nothing like a warm shower," he said.

A tall boy, standing under the next faucet, turned. "You can say that again," he said. "I feel I want to stay under here all day."

Bobby grinned. "My name is Bobby Reynolds," he offered.

"Mine is Charlie Lewis. Nice to meet you, even if it is under water."

Bobby laughed. "You a rookie?" he asked.

"Yes. I play second base. This is my first time at training camp with the Sox. You are the bonus kid, aren't you? First time for you, too?"

"Yes," Bobby said. "First time. I signed my contract last June, after high-school graduation. I was still in school during spring training. I played half a season with Oakmont, but I wasn't with the Sox."

Bobby turned off the water. He heard loud laughter coming from the locker room. "Wonder what is going on," he said.

"Must be those two funny fellows who room together," Charlie said. "They were starting in when I came in here."

"Who are they?"

"Roger Saltin and Louie Ziller. Remember that big magazine story about them last year? They called it something like Baseball's Strangest Roommates."

Bobby remembered reading the story. He smiled and said, "Saltin is the Yale University graduate. Real smart, isn't he?"

"Right," Charlie said. "And Ziller is the guy who never finished high school. They are always picking on each other."

"I'm going to see them in action," Bobby said. "See you later."

Bobby dried himself. "Charlie Lewis seems like a nice guy," he thought. He wrapped the towel around him and walked into the locker room. There, he joined the ball players who were surrounding the rubbing table. Bobby edged in close to hear what was going on.

"Louie," Saltin was saying. "You are making a joke out of the English language, a parody."

"I'm making a what of it?" Ziller said.

"A parody. A burlesque. A farce. You are making fun of it."

"How do you like that?" Louie said. "I always thought a parody was one of those little birds you can teach to talk."

Saltin threw up his hands in disgust. The Sox roared.

"Come on, I am not so dumb," Louie said. "You went to college to learn those big words and it cost your old man a mint of money. Now I just sit around and learn all your knowledge for nothing."

The Sox roared again. Bobby scratched his head. It seemed funny that such different fellows could room with each other. "I guess Ziller really isn't so dumb," Bobby thought.

Manager O'Connor rubbed tears of laughter from his eyes. "Those two are the funniest pair since Yogi Berra and Bobby Brown," Yank said.

"They are funnier," Coach Templeton said.

"Impossible," Yank said. "Remember the time Yogi and Bobby were catching up on their reading before going to bed? Yogi was reading a comic book and Bobby, who was studying to be a doctor, was reading a book about medicine. Well, Yogi finishes and puts his comic book on the bedside table. Then Brown closes his book and puts it away, too. Superman did it again, Yogi said. How did your book come out?"

O'Connor and Templeton laughed some more. Bobby walked to his locker, grinning to himself.

He had heard the story before, but he always got a big kick out of it.

At dinner that night Bobby and Tony were talking about their chances of sticking with the Sox. "We both have pretty tough jobs," Bobby said. "You have to beat out Sunderlin at shortstop, and I have to beat out Regan in centerfield."

"I know," Tony said. "But I want to make good so much that I would cut off my right arm to stick with the Sox.

"You know what I mean," he continued. "I have been dreaming about this since I was a little kid."

The waiter put two hot platters on the table and the boys started to eat. Bobby dug a fork into his medium-rare steak to see if it was tender. But before cutting into it, he ate all of his potatoes and string beans. Ever since he could remember, he had eaten the vegetables on his plate before tasting the meat.

"Watch me tomorrow," Tony said. "I'll move so fast, I will knock them dead."

Bobby reached for the bread. "Don't you think you should take it easy at first," he said. "You might get hurt before you even get started."

Tony frowned. "When you are a rookie, you have to go full steam from the beginning," he said. "If nobody notices you right away, you can be back in the minor league in the first month."

"I guess they have been noticing me all right,"

Bobby said. "Those men with the cameras really had me jumping today."

"If I were you, Bobby, I would try to take it easy with that kind of stuff. I heard a couple of the older fellows talking today. They are boiling mad because of all the attention you are getting. They were saying that if the Sox wanted to hire someone who would look good in pictures, they should have signed Tab Hunter."

Bobby stared at his plate. "But what can I do? If I don't do what they ask, I'll get the writers and the others down on me."

"And if you do," Tony replied, "you get the players down on you."

"What is the answer?"

"I don't know. But that is a problem I wouldn't mind having—so long as I had the $60,000 that went with it."

Later that night, Bobby twisted and turned in his bed, wanting to fall asleep. His legs ached from the exercises, but his mind whirled with worries. "All I am trying to do is what I'm asked," he thought, "and the guys are getting sore at me. I wonder what I should do. If I were just another rookie, nobody would be angry with me. Nobody is angry with Tony, or with Charlie Lewis. But they didn't get the $60,000. I did. That bonus may be the hardest thing I will ever have to live down."

chapter 4

SWINGING FOR THE FENCES

The sun-baked ground crunched beneath Bobby's
spikes as he trotted across the grass. His arms swung
in a lazy way. He was saving up energy. So were the
other players. Suddenly, Yank O'Connor's booming
voice sounded on the field.

"Come on, you hitters," Yank yelled. "Get in here
and take your swings at that ball. Let's go! Let's
go! We don't have all year."

"He never lets up, does he?" Bobby said, digging
his right toe into the dirt and turning on the speed.

Tenda, running beside Bobby, frowned. "The first
$60,000 may have come easy, Golden Boy," he said,
"but from now on, you have to earn your money,
like the rest of us."

38

Yank's voice boomed again. "Saltin and Robinson stay here. The rest of you pitchers go out in the field and run. And keep running until I say stop. Which may not be until tomorrow unless I see that fat dripping off."

Spring training was moving into full swing at the Sox camp. The extra pounds were pouring off the sweating ball players. The first few days had been set aside for exercises, running and batting practice against Iron Mike, the pitching machine. Now it was time for more important work. Bobby was running in with the first wave of players who would hit against live pitchers.

A handful of Sox lined up outside the batting cage. Bobby watched Tenda walk forward, swinging at the air with three bats. "Come on, big man," Ziller said. "Get going with another big season."

Tenda dropped two of the bats and stepped into the cage. He stood deep in the batter's box, his right foot planted firmly at the end chalk line and his left foot pointed toward the shortstop. He held the bat high, his elbows on a line with the letters on his uniform shirt. The hundred or so fans in the creaking wooden stands leaned forward.

On the mound, Phil Robinson pulled on his cap, wound up and threw a medium-speed pitch. Tenda met the ball squarely. His swing drove it against the leftfield fence. Seven more times, Robinson sent the ball over the heart of the plate. Five of those times, Tenda drove it against the fence, rattling the boards. Once, he hit the ball over the fence.

Tenda grinned as he stepped out of the batting cage. Regan moved up to hit next, but Tenda planted a heavy hand on Barry's chest.

"Let the Golden Boy up next," Tom said. "I want to see him match me."

Bobby wrapped two fingers around his gold ring and twisted until it ate into his skin. He had been wearing the ring since his junior year in high school. "Remember to take it off when you play ball," his dad had said when he gave the ring to Bobby. "It will interfere with your grip on the bat."

But Bobby had forgotten to take it off and the first time he wore it in a ball game, he hit a booming home run. Since then, he had been wearing it all the time, on and off the field.

Bobby pressed the ring hard as he stepped into the batter's box. He smoothed the dirt carefully with his feet and tugged at his cap. He held his bat high, like Tenda. But Bobby was a lefthanded hitter.

Bobby swung full force at Robinson's first pitch and hit a lazy pop-up. He banged the handle of the bat against his spikes and dug in tighter.

Robinson sent another pitch over the middle and Bobby missed it. The force of the swing whirled him around, snapping the cap off his head.

Yank O'Connor frowned, multiplying the wrinkles on his face. "Swinging for the fences," Yank said to Templeton. "He won't go anywhere doing that."

Only once did Bobby connect with the ball. He hit the fence in right-center. But he missed five pitches, hit one pop-up and one ground ball.

He hit a grounder on his eighth swing. Then he turned to batting-practice catcher, Sammy Gordon. "How many is that?" Bobby asked. "Six?"

"Six!" yelled Sunderlin. "If you stay in there much longer, it will be sundown."

Regan shot a stream of tobacco juice to the ground. "Come on, Reynolds," he said. "The rest of us want to hit, too."

"If you don't mind, that is," Tenda said, bowing in the direction of Bobby.

The next day, with two runners on base and two out in the sixth inning of a practice game, Bobby swung wildly at a fast ball and missed. Then he connected with a curve and sent it high over the center-field fence.

At the crack of the bat, Speed Peters raced down the stairs and out of the park. Speed circled the outside of the stadium until he reached the spot where he thought the ball might have landed. He walked up to a small boy who was holding a baseball.

"Did that ball just come over the fence?" Speed asked.

"Yes, sir. Can't I keep it? We always keep the balls that come over the fence."

"Sure, sure. You can keep it. Here, keep this one, too." Speed reached into his pocket and handed the boy a ball signed by all the Sox.

"Wow! Thanks."

"All I want you to do is show me where the ball landed," Speed said.

"Yes, sir. Sure."

The boy ran about 100 feet from the fence. "Right here, sir."

Speed beamed. "Great," he said. "Just great! Ball goes 450 feet over the fence and another 100 outside until it bounces. That is my big story today."

Speed returned and passed along the news to the writers. "I told you this kid is the next Babe Ruth," he said. "How about that? A 550-foot homer."

The next day, the sports pages were full of stories about Bobby Reynolds, the new baseball wonder. A story by Paul Keller ended with these words:

"Those of us who have spent some time writing about baseball have seen many young men rise up in the spring, only to plunge sadly to earth in the summer. But we have seen few fellows with as much promise as young Bobby Reynolds. He runs with the speed of a deer, he fields with skill and he hits a baseball with as much power as any man who has ever played the game.

"The two greatest rookies I have seen were Frank Howard and Mickey Mantle. The third is Bobby Reynolds. I would not be surprised if Reynolds went on to become the best of them all."

Most of the Sox players read Paul Keller's story with interest before they went down to breakfast.

But Bobby and Tony were too busy to pick up the paper that was left outside their door. The radio was playing full blast in their hotel room and they were jumping with the early morning music.

"Great music, simply great," Bobby said, bouncing in time to the music.

"I've got this record," Tony said. He drummed the beat with his fingertips. "I know every note."

"I've got it, too," Bobby said.

"Let's hear," Tony said. "Take the trumpet part."

Bobby held his left fist against his mouth and held his right hand out front, palm open. His fingers snapped at the air and he sang in time to the music. "Da, da, dee, dum! Da, da, dee, dum!"

"I will take the saxophone part," Tony called. He tucked his left hand under his chin, and held his right hand a few inches from his stomach. His black hair fell over his forehead as he bounced his body. He moved his fingers as though he were touching saxophone keys. "Boop, boop, boop," he sung out deep.

Bobby fell to one knee and lifted his head and hands high. "Dum, dum, dee."

Tony slid to both knees, waving his hands. "Boop, boop, boop."

A commercial cut short the music. The boys beamed. "I didn't know you could play a trumpet," Tony said.

"That makes us even," Bobby said. "I didn't know you could play a saxophone."

"Neither did I," Tony said.

The boys laughed and rushed for the newspaper. Tony pounced upon it first. He grabbed it, opened it up to the sports pages and spread them on the living-room floor. The boys read Paul Keller's story. They were quiet. Finally, Tony snapped his fingers.

"Nice story," he said. "He has given you a lot to live up to."

"Maybe too much," Bobby said. He stared at his ring. "Nothing I can do but try."

Bobby tried. In the practice game that afternoon, he tried too hard. He swung for the fences each time he was at bat and he struck out four times. After the fourth time, he slammed the bat handle against his spikes with such force that he splintered the wood. Manager O'Connor watched the wood break. Then he called Bobby over.

"If you keep swinging for those fences," Yank said, "you will swing yourself right back to Oakmont. Forget about home runs. Go for singles. Just get your bat on the ball. With your strong wrists and your power, the ball will jump out of the park."

"Yes, sir, I'll remember," Bobby said.

Bobby ran to the locker room. He put a bear hug on Tony. "Tony," he said. "You want to help me make the Sox?"

"Sure," Tony said.

"Good. When I go up to bat, you whistle or yell or clap your hands. Anything to remind me to swing easy."

Tony grinned. "And if that doesn't work," he said, "I'll tie the bat to your shoulder. Now let go of me before you squeeze me to death."

Tony tried every way he knew how to help Bobby. He whistled. He yelled. He clapped. But Bobby could not hit, day after day of practice. For a week, he went with nothing but pop-ups and easy grounders.

Bobby blinked in surprise when he saw his name listed in the starting lineup for the Sox exhibition

game before the start of the regular ball season. Tenda roared with surprise. "I guess O'Connor must be reading the papers," the catcher said. "He certainly wasn't watching practice."

"What are you complaining about?" Saltin asked him. "You didn't become a big star overnight either."

"Right," Tenda said. "I spent six years learning how to play big-league ball. No one paid me big money until I began socking home runs for the Sox. Nobody gave me $60,000 because they thought I might be a star some day."

"Well, Reynolds was lucky enough to get the money and that's that," Saltin said. "If he can help us win the pennant, I am all for him."

Tenda's face grew dark. "I am all for him, too, if he can do that," Tom said. "But the way he has been playing, he doesn't look as though he could help a

Little League team win a pennant, much less us."

Bobby, Tony and Ziller walked by as Tenda was finishing. "Don't listen to him, kid," Ziller said. "He has been steamed up all spring."

Bobby nodded, but inside him anger boiled. He grabbed his uniform off the locker hooks. "I will show them today," he said to Tony. "I will hit the ball so far they will never find it."

When the players trotted onto the field, the fans crowded against the chicken-wire fence for a closer look. It was the usual spring-training audience. The men were comfortably dressed in sport shirts and slacks. Most of the girls, women and boys wore shorts.

Three teen-age girls pressed their noses against the fence behind first base. "There is Bobby Reynolds," they screamed together.

"Bobby, Bobby," the prettiest of the three yelled. "Hit a home run for me."

"I'd like to hit one for myself," Bobby told Tony.

Bobby struck out his first two times at bat. The other Sox were not doing much, either. At the end of four innings, the Bombers led, 2–0, and Lard Jennings came in to pitch for the Sox.

Lard allowed no runs in the fifth and the sixth. Usually, his best pitch was his knuckle ball and today it was too much for the Bombers. In the bottom of the sixth, Tenda hit a home run, but Bobby, who was after him, popped out to the shortstop. The one run made the score 2–1 in favor of the Bombers going into the last half of the ninth inning.

With two out, Bobby waited his turn and watched Tenda at bat. Crack! Bobby jumped up as the big catcher connected with a curve ball. The ball flew over the fence. Tenda had his second home run of the day and a tie score, 2–2, when Bobby walked to the plate. His handsome face was serious. He twisted his ring, rubbed his hands in the dirt and dug in. Tony's sharp whistle cut through the air. Bobby's grip became loose on the bat.

Bink Sanders wound up and fired a high, fast ball. Bobby reached for it and hit it hard. The ball flew out to centerfield. It cleared the fence with yards to

spare. Bobby looked around and grinned at Tony.

"What a shot!" Speed Peters yelled to the newspaper writers watching the game in the press box. "That is better than the one he hit two weeks ago."

"How far do you think it went, Speed?" Paul Keller asked.

"Easy 550, maybe 600," Speed said.

"Let's call it 575."

"Fair enough," Speed said.

Bobby stepped on home plate, then raced happily for the dressing room through the dugout's open door and ran head first into Marvin Gillette, a writer for the Cleveland *Gazette*. Marvin fell into an open locker, his notebook flying to the top shelf.

Bobby reached over and lifted him up. "Sorry," Bobby said.

"That's okay," Marvin said. "You are just the man I want to see."

He backed Bobby into a corner. "That the longest ball you ever hit?"

"Gee, I don't know. I don't think so," Bobby said.

Marvin glanced up and saw the other writers walking toward the lockers. "I have some questions I would like you to answer quickly," he said.

"Okay," said Bobby.

"At Oakmont last year, you hit 35 home runs in 75 games. That is about half the season, right?"

"Right."

49

"Well, I figure that if you had played the full season, hitting like that, you would have had twice as many home runs, right?"

"Right, in a way," Bobby said.

"Twice 35 is 70, right?"

"Right."

Gillette pulled out a sheet of paper. "Tenda played six years in the minors," he said, "and he hit a total of 68 homers. So if you could have had your 70, you would have hit more home runs in one season than Tom hit in six seasons, right?"

"If I had hit 70, I guess that would be right."

"Thanks," Marvin said. "You just gave me a great story."

"Did I?" Bobby said, surprised.

In the *Gazette* the following day, Gillette wrote, "Not only does young Bobby Reynolds hit with great power, but he is full of stories, too. 'I hit 35 homers in half a season at Oakmont last year,' Bobby told me yesterday, 'and if I had played the full season, it would have been 70.'

"Bobby then added, 'That would have given me more homers in one minor-league season than Tenda hit in six.'"

Roger Saltin slapped the *Gazette* to the floor.

"What a shame," Saltin said. "Every time that young man opens his mouth, he seems to put his foot squarely in it."

chapter 5

"I'M RUNNING THIS CLUB"

The big morning had arrived. The Sox were leaving Saint Petersburg, heading home to Cleveland. Bobby was up at seven o'clock. He snapped off the alarm and walked quietly around the room. "No sense waking Tony," he said to himself. "We don't leave for another three hours."

Bobby stuffed clothes into his suitcase and stacked it up against Tony's, which had been packed the night before. Then he closed the door quietly, walked to the hotel coffee shop for a quick breakfast, and then walked for an hour along Saint Petersburg's tree-lined streets.

Bobby wanted to be alone, to think hard, to try to understand what had been happening to him.

"Ever since I hit that homer," he said to himself, "everything has been going wrong. I can't make friends with any of the older players. They have been angry with me ever since Gillette wrote that story."

Bobby could understand why the players were angry. "I guess that is what Speed meant when he told me to be careful with the writers," he thought. "I have tried to explain to the players that Gillette said all those words, not me. But all they do is say, 'Yes, of course, Mr. Reynolds, sir.'"

It was no wonder that Tenda had stormed up to Tony the day the story appeared in the paper. "Tell your rich friend that if he sounds off like that again, I will punch him right in the nose," Tenda had said.

Bobby could understand, too, why Regan, Robinson and Sunderlin had surrounded him in the steaming shower room one day and really let loose. "Mr. Reynolds, sir," Robinson had said, "I understand you have been elected to the Hall of Fame."

"Mr. Reynolds, sir," Sunderlin had said, "you are 261 major-league home runs behind Tenda. Do you think you will pass him this year?"

To make matters worse, Bobby had fallen into Manager Yank O'Connor's doghouse. "I know he wants me to swing easy," Bobby thought, as he walked along the streets, "but I have to prove myself. If I don't swing hard, I won't get any hits at all."

Bobby stuffed his hands in his pockets. His fingers

wrapped around an envelope. It was a letter from his dad.

Bobby had written to his father to tell him some of his problems. "Everything I do ends up wrong," Bobby had written. "I can't make friends, I can't hit and the newspaper men still keep writing about how great I am going to be. I don't know what to do. Maybe you shouldn't have taught me how to be a ball player. Maybe I should never have even started to play this game."

For the tenth time, Bobby opened the envelope and read his dad's answer. "I can't help but think you are feeling sorry for yourself," his father wrote. "If you are, then I have no sympathy for you." Bobby could almost hear his dad's deep voice. "What you have to do now is hold up your head and pay no attention to the players. If the riding gets too bad, just stand up for your rights."

Bobby looked up into the sun. Dad is right, he thought. I know he is right. I won't pay attention to the other players if I can help it, but then, if I have to, I will fight back, even with my fists.

The thought of fist-fighting sent a shiver up Bobby's spine, in spite of the warm sun. Once, in a high school baseball game, he had run in from the outfield to try to break up a fight. Before he could pull the boys apart, a fellow from the other team had punched him in the jaw. Bobby had brought back his fist and fired it at the boy. The punch had landed hard, breaking the boy's nose. Bobby had vowed right then that he never would lose his temper like that again, and he had not.

The sun beat down on Bobby's face. "But if I have to fight," he said aloud, "I will."

Bobby dropped onto one of the wooden benches which line the Saint Petersburg streets. A small white card was lying at the edge of the walk. An ant made its way across the walk. Bobby stretched his feet and pushed the white card in the way of the ant. He watched the insect consider the card, then start to go around it.

With his foot Bobby moved the card and again blocked the path of the ant. Again the ant began to circle the card.

Three more times, Bobby blocked the ant's path. Each time the ant found a way to get around the card. Suddenly, Bobby thought, "Here I am putting things in that ant's way just to see if it can go around them. Maybe that is what has been happening to me. Heck, if a little ant can get around things that are in his way, certainly I can."

Bobby burst into the hotel room, exploding with energy. He stopped short when he saw Tony in the desk chair. "What's the matter, Tony?" Bobby said. "Get a move on. We are leaving in a couple of minutes. I mean it. Hurry up."

"You are leaving," Tony said. "Me, I am not going anywhere today."

"What do you mean?"

"I have been sent down, that's what I mean. To the minors. I fly to Oakmont tomorrow."

Bobby felt his knees buckle. "Nobody wanted to make good any more than Tony," he thought. "Nobody tried harder. It was terrible."

Bobby tried to force a smile. "You will be back, Tony," he said. "Sure, you'll be back real soon."

"I hope so," Tony said. Then he was on his feet. "Look, Bobby, you knock them dead, you hear. Hit those big homers for both of us." Tony paused and whistled. "And with an easy swing, you hear, an easy swing."

"What a guy," Bobby thought. "Here he is going down to the minors and thinking of me. I wish there were some way I could help him."

Bobby knew that the truth was there was nothing he could do to help his friend. He put his arm around Tony and slapped him on the back. "You are too good to stay in the minors."

Bobby grabbed his suitcase and waved goodby. He wanted to stay and try to cheer up Tony, but he had to be on the team bus. He got on alone, thinking of Tony. Most of the other players were edged forward on their seats, laughing.

"Those two," Bobby said to himself. "They are at

it again. Roger Saltin and Louie Ziller are at it again."

"Louie," Saltin was saying. "Plato was a famous teacher who lived in Greece hundreds of years ago."

"No, sir," Ziller said. "This is one time you can't fool me. I know darn well who Plato is. He is Mickey Mouse's dog."

Saltin threw his arms up in the air and the ball players roared. "You tell him, Louie," Regan laughed. "Nobody can put one over on you."

The first stop for the Sox on their swing north was Jacksonville, Florida. The night game there against the National League Birds was the beginning of what Bobby had heard the ball players call "the money ride home."

Bobby knew that on "the money ride home"

rookies like himself and Charlie Lewis had to prove they were big leaguers. The regular players, already set in their jobs, had to practice until they were at their best. The old-timers, who knew in their hearts that they were almost through, had to battle for another year of big salary. They fought the hardest.

One such old-timer was Lard Jennings. In 12 seasons with the Sox, Lard had pitched 191 victories. When the Sox won their last pennant, seven years before, Lard had been the biggest star. He won 27 regular season games that year and added two victories in the World Series.

Lard had been a relief pitcher the last couple of seasons, using his experience to get out the batters he once struck out with fast balls. The Sox were certain that Lard could not last much longer, and his work in spring-training camp had done little to change their minds. Except for the game he won against the Bombers, Jennings had not helped the Sox, or himself, one bit.

The fans in the Jacksonville ball park shouted wildly when Lard Jennings was called in to pitch in the seventh inning. Bobby knew why. They had come to the park expecting to see a high-scoring spring training game, but instead, had been treated to seven innings of very good baseball. There had been great pitching and fielding and the score was tied, 1–1. The fans guessed that Jennings was battling for his big-league life, due to his age.

For three innings, Jennings' knuckle ball fooled the Bird batters. They swung hard, but could not connect. The ball always seemed to dance away at the last second. The Sox could not get any more runs either, and they came up in the bottom of the ninth with the score still tied.

Bobby sat on the hard wooden bench in the dugout, twisting his ring. He watched Regan stuff a plug of tobacco into his jaw. "Get them, gang," Regan yelled. "Get it over with."

"Come on, big Tom," Ziller said. "Homer wins it for us."

Tenda wrapped his hands around the warm-up bat and twisted hard. "He looks as if he wants to squeeze out the lead filling," Bobby thought. Tenda swung it a couple of times, then picked up the big, brown bat with which he would hit. He stepped in the batter's box and sent a single to rightfield.

Bobby listened to the stands buzz with excitement as Joe Fenton, the hard-hitting but slow-running rightfielder, came to bat next and tapped a grounder to the Bomber second baseman. "A sure double play," Bobby thought. "A sure double play."

The second baseman threw to the shortstop. Tenda was out. The throw back to first base was a split second too late. Fenton stepped on the bag ahead of the ball. He was safe.

Yank O'Connor stood up and wrinkled his nose, then tugged at his cap, planning his next move. He looked up and down the bench. His cold stare settled on Bobby. "Reynolds," he boomed, "get in and run for Fenton."

Bobby made sure his shoe laces were tightly tied, then ran out to first base and set his left foot against the bag. He looked across the field and checked signs with the third-base coach, Templeton.

The coach rubbed his hands along the letters of his shirt, then touched his right ear. It was the Sox sign to steal, to try to run to second before the catcher could throw him out.

Bobby dug his right toe into the ground and took a long lead. Willie Reel, the Birds' pitcher, looked over, then turned toward the plate. As Reel's arm swung toward the plate, Bobby dashed for second. He slid hard, hooking the inside corner of the bag ahead of the shortstop's sweeping tag.

Regan hit Reel's next pitch on the ground toward second. He was thrown out easily at first, but Bobby advanced to third.

Bobby stood on the base, staring at Templeton. Again the coach rubbed the letters on his shirt and touched his right ear. The steal sign again, this time to race to home plate ahead of the throw, the most difficult of all steals. Bobby gritted his teeth, dug his toe into the dirt and edged off the bag.

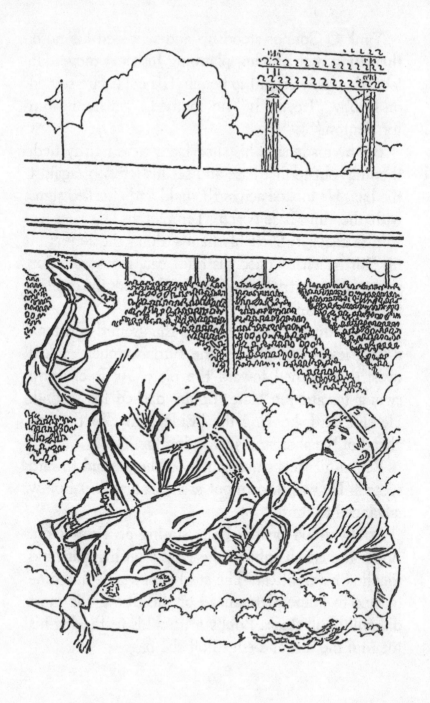

Reel went into a full windup, paying no attention to the runner. As soon as the pitcher kicked back, Bobby flew toward the plate. Reel quickly threw home.

The ball and Bobby arrived at almost the same second. Bobby slid in with the full fury of his 220 pounds. The Birds' catcher leaned in to catch the ball, but he tumbled right over Bobby, unable to make a tag. The run scored, the game was over and the Sox had won.

Bobby leaped up and ran for the dressing room. When he reached his locker, Jennings was waiting for him.

"Thank you, son," Lard said. "I don't think I could have lasted another inning. I might have wasted all my good work."

Bobby grinned. For the first time in two weeks an older player had said a kind word to him.

For the remainder of the trip north, Manager O'Connor worked Bobby into every game. Regan played centerfield for the first six innings; Bobby took over in the final three. Bobby began to hit the ball again, not well all the time, but hard and very long when he did connect. Against the Bombers in Athens, Georgia, Bobby hit a home run that traveled almost 550 feet. Against the Bengals in Charlotte, North Carolina, he smashed a line drive so hard that it ripped the glove off the third baseman's hand.

Three days before the season was to open, Fenton hurt his knee sliding into second base. Doc Tanner, the club doctor, examined the knee and said that Joe would be out for at least two weeks.

On the rocking, speeding train bound for Cleveland that night, O'Connor told the newspaper men that Bobby Reynolds would open the season in rightfield. "If he does okay," Yank said, "we may very well keep him with us all season."

The writers, led by Keller and Gillette, rushed to the dining car to tell Bobby the good news. "Rightfield?" Bobby said. "I haven't played rightfield since I was eleven years old."

"You mean you don't want to play there?" Gillette asked.

Bobby stared at the ceiling. He did not know what he wanted. He could not believe it. It did not make sense. He was a centerfielder. He really had not played rightfield since he was 11. He thought about the different throwing angles from rightfield. He thought about the funny way the sun and shadows hit it. He didn't know how to play there. He was even a little scared to try. If he had practiced there all spring, it would have been different.

"No, I would like not to play rightfield," he said. "I'm a centerfielder. I know how to play centerfield, but I'm not used to right. Yank says that if I do well, I will stick with the Sox all year. Well, if he wants me to play well, I would like to play my regular position. I'm a centerfielder. Wouldn't that be better?"

The writers looked at each other with surprise. They had their story for the day. How often did a rookie speak up against his manager? They hurried to their typewriters. The train roared on toward Cleveland.

Bobby and Charlie Lewis spent the next day in Cleveland, putting a fresh coat of paint on the three-room furnished apartment that had been rented for them.

"We may be here all season and we may only be here a week," Charlie said, "but we should get the place looking nice anyway."

"Sure," Bobby said. "It will really begin feeling like home when Mom sends my record player and records. Wait until you hear my Brubecks."

Charlie began mixing the paint and Bobby piled the furniture in the center of the room. "Let's start with the ceiling," Charlie said, handing Bobby a paint brush.

Soon, Bobby had smeared more white paint on his hair and T-shirt than on the ceiling.

"Stay away from me," Charlie said, laughing. "You will paint me white, too."

Charlie pushed Bobby toward the windows. "Work over here," he said. "Far away. Why don't you paint the window trim?"

Bobby looked at the narrow strips of wood around the glass panes. "Are you kidding?" he said. "I will paint the glass all white. Why don't you let me paint that big wall. That's more my style."

"Okay, just stay far from me."

Late that afternoon, Charlie suggested they call the Sox office to find out if they had any messages. "We should do that every day," he said, "until our phone is in."

Bobby agreed and they walked down the street to a drug store. Young boys passed, dressed in Little League uniforms and carrying bats and gloves.

One of the Little Leaguers swung a brown bat around his shoulders. "Boom," he yelled. "Home run. Just like Bobby Reynolds."

Charlie planted an elbow in Bobby's ribs. "Go over and introduce yourself," he said.

"No, thanks," Bobby said. "Be happy they didn't know us. We would have had to sign our names about 20 times."

Charlie changed a quarter in the drug store and slid into a phone booth. He slid out a few minutes later, a strange look on his face.

"We have a couple of letters waiting for us," he said, "and you have an important message. O'Connor wants to see you immediately. Speed says the old man is really mad."

Back at the apartment, Bobby showered and

changed into a neat three-button blue suit, white shirt, and red and blue striped tie. He stood on the sidewalk, staring at the light shining from his ring. He was pretty sure he had put his foot in his mouth again. When Bobby arrived at the Sox downtown offices, Speed Peters came out to meet him in the waiting room.

"Are you nuts, boy?" Speed said. "Why did you want to go and sound off about rightfield like that? Didn't I tell you to be careful with the writers?"

"I know you told me. I forgot. I didn't realize what I was doing. I just got scared at the thought of playing rightfield and said what came into my head. I just didn't think."

Speed pointed to a walnut door. "It's your party," he said. "The old man is waiting for you in there."

O'Connor greeted Bobby by pounding a paper weight against the desk. "Before you open up your big mouth," Yank said, "let's get one thing straight. I am the manager. I am running this ball club. You are not running this ball club. Tom Tenda is not running this ball club. The writers aren't running this ball club. I am running it.

"You will play anywhere I tell you to play, sonny. That may be centerfield, that may be rightfield or that may very well be Oakmont. Now get out of here before I really lose my temper."

chapter 6

THE BONUS BUST

It was the evening before the first game of the regular season. Big-league teams can have only 25 players on the team after a certain date and it is the manager's place to decide, during spring training and exhibition games, which players should be sent to the minor league in order to keep the team down to the limit. Although the Sox did not have to decide until a month later what players to drop from the team, General Manager Alexander believed in trimming the list of players before opening day.

"There is no sense in keeping players around just to decorate the bench," he always explained. "By sending them down to the minor leagues in April, we give them an extra month of real play."

Harry Lawrence, the man in charge of the Sox farm teams, opened the talks. Harry sat at one end of the table with O'Connor and Alexander on either side of him.

"If we keep Bobby Reynolds here any longer," Harry said, "we will only hurt him. Sure, he has hit some long home runs. But he has struck out a lot more times than he has hit the ball. I can't see that it will do him any good to play a few weeks with the big club, then be sent down looking like a wash out. It will be better for him this way."

Alexander nodded his gray head. Coach O'Connor stared straight ahead, his face still.

"I agree with Harry," Alexander said. "It is too much to risk. We have $60,000 tied up in this kid and he can be worth it, too. But if he keeps going the way he has been, striking out and making more trouble with the players and Yank, he will be washed up. If we ship him to Oakmont now, he can get straightened out."

O'Connor, who only the day before had been so angry with Bobby, shook his head. "You both have got it wrong," Yank said. "Sending him down now is what will hurt the kid. He can hit well enough to help us. It is only in his head that he has trouble. I think we can get him over it, and I think we should go all the way and try it."

"How about the other players?" Alexander said.

"Can he get along with them, I want to know?"

"He has to learn how to get along with them, and he might as well learn now," Yank said. "If we send him down, he will have the same problem with the players next year. All he has to do to shut them up is to start hitting."

The manager sat down, his eyes narrowed. Yank was 60 years old and he had been around baseball for a long time. The two other men at the table believed in him. They finally agreed to keep Reynolds with the Sox.

Charlie Lewis made the team, too. Both of the rookies were in the starting lineup on opening day. Charlie was at second base, batting eighth against the Bombers. Bobby was in rightfield, batting fifth.

Having to play rightfield no longer bothered Bobby. All he wanted was the chance to prove he could be a good teammate for the Sox. Yank himself had no grudge. "Those things happen," he had explained to Coach Templeton. "If anything, Reynolds will play better because of it."

What Yank said made sense, but it did not work out. Opening day, Bobby came up to bat three times with men on base and not once could he deliver a hit. A double by Tenda and a home run by leftfielder Warren Groten saved the Sox from being shut out, but the team lost, 5–2.

All week, Bobby swung wildly. He made only four

68

hits—three singles and a double—in 21 times at bat. Tenda and Regan were hitting the ball hard, though, and the Sox were in first place, one game ahead of the Bengals.

In the opener of a three-game series against the Bears in Chicago, O'Connor dropped Bobby to seventh in the lineup. Instead of making Bobby relax, it made him try harder. In the next game he struck out twice and popped up twice.

That night, Bobby and Charlie Lewis sat in the Rose Top Hotel, talking over their troubles.

"I guess we're the two worst hitters in the league," Charlie said. "We can't buy a base hit."

"But at least you are making great plays in the field," Bobby said.

"You can snap out of it," Charlie said. "Heck, you hit these same pitchers in spring training."

"I'm hitting .160," Bobby said. "Imagine— .160."

"And I'm hitting .220," Charlie said. "What is so good about that?"

The boys did not know that Tenda and Regan were sitting right behind them, listening to every word. Suddenly, Tenda spoke up.

"If I were that Reynolds kid," Tom said, "I would put my money in the bank and get a job somewhere else. That way I wouldn't be hurting my team's chances to win a pennant."

"I dunno," Regan said. He couldn't chew tobacco on the main floor of the hotel, so he had a big, black cigar. He waved it as he spoke. "If he swings a hammer as wildly as he swings a bat, he is likely to break all his fingers."

"Could be," Tom said. "Say, Barry, have you noticed how nobody in the newspapers seems to be writing about Mr. Reynolds any more?"

"I certainly have," Regan said. "What a shame. I was keeping a scrap book about him and it is only half full."

Bobby's face flushed with anger. He began to rise. Charlie grabbed his arm. "Show them you can take it," Charlie whispered, "or they will never let up."

"I don't think they ever want to, no matter what I do," Bobby said.

"Just be quiet. Come on. Hey, let's go get something to eat."

"We just ate."

"Well, let's go eat again. All of a sudden, I am starving. If I don't eat soon, I might get sick. You have no idea how hungry I am."

A broad grin spread over Bobby's sun-tanned face. "Okay," he said. "You're right, Charlie. Thanks."

Bobby and Charlie stood up and walked slowly to the hotel entrance. They passed Sunderlin. The shortstop ground a cigarette into a marble ashtray and greeted Charlie warmly. "Hi, Charlie," he said.

"Great play you made on Ballantine today."

Then Sunderlin bowed low. "Why, good evening, Mr. Reynolds," he said. "How are you, sir?"

Bobby paid no attention to him, staring straight ahead at a red and green sign. FLY TO SUNNY CALIFORNIA, it read in big, bold letters. YOUR JET GETS YOU THERE IN FOUR HOURS.

"I may just be doing that soon," Bobby thought. "Flying a jet to Oakmont."

The trip to Oakmont grew more real in Bobby's mind the next afternoon. He did not play in the game at all. He sat unhappily on the bench. "I guess I'm really through," he thought.

That night, Bobby read a postcard from his spring-training pal, Tony Luco. "Things are going good in Oakmont," Tony wrote. "Hope to see you soon—in the big leagues."

"I hope so," Bobby thought. "But it looks more as though I would see you in Oakmont."

On Sunday, Bobby was back in the lineup. He did not make any hits, but with two out and two Bears on base in the seventh inning, Jim Redding hit a low line drive to right-center. Both runners were off with the crack of the bat. So was rightfielder Reynolds.

"Double, double," screamed Lou Gallagher. He jumped up and down in the Bears' coaching box like a boy who had just received a Christmas present.

"He can't get it," Yank said, racing to the dugout steps. "Sure two runs."

Bobby ran like a deer toward the sinking ball. Finally, he flung himself straight across the grass, stretching out his glove as far as his long left arm could reach. He scooped in the ball before it touched the top of the grass and tumbled over in a full somersault.

Redding ground to a halt at second base and kicked the dust out of the bag. "Greatest catch I ever saw," he said, "and it had to happen on my hit."

Later, in the dressing room, Tenda stood in front of his locker. A twisted smile was on his hard face. "Yes, sir," he said, "they pay real big money for acrobats these days."

All of the players heard Tom. Regan and Sunderlin laughed. Saltin wrinkled up his nose. Lard Jennings waited until Bobby went into the shower. Then he walked over to Tenda's locker.

"Don't you think you are being pretty pigheaded," Lard said. "The kid saved the game for us."

"Oh, come on," Tom said. "We would have won anyway. Look, I am not forgetting the crack he made about me in spring training."

"How do you know he really said that? You know how a kid can get mixed up with newspaper writers."

"Well, why didn't he say he was sorry or explain

73

it? Because he couldn't explain it, that's why."

"Explain to you? Every time he comes within ten yards of you, you wise off."

"Look, you are the only guy he has helped on the ball field, so it figures you would defend him. As far as I know, and as far as most of the boys know, he has been hurting us. If he had made just a couple of key hits, we could be way out in front now. You have been around a long time. You know how important it is to win these early games. Just as important as winning them late in the season. I think everybody would be a lot happier if the Sox split up that $60,000 among the guys who are helping this club, and put that kid out to pasture."

Louie Ziller elbowed in between Jennings and Tenda. "Come on, you guys," Louie said. "This is a ball club. We stick together, remember?"

"You are right, Louie," Tom said. "I'm sorry, Lard. We have been friends for years. Let's not let this bonus kid break us up."

On the plane back to Cleveland that night, Charlie told Bobby about the argument in the dressing room. "I thought sure as shooting Lard was going to sock him. And Roger Saltin was on your side, too. I could tell. See, Bobby? You have a lot of friends on this team."

"Maybe five guys," Bobby said. "And I need every one of them."

Thousands of Sox fans were Bobby's friends, too. The newspaper reports out of spring training had built him up as a combination of Babe Ruth and Mickey Mantle. The fans were sure that Bobby could bring them a pennant. They fell in love with him before they even saw him swing a bat.

For a long time, Cleveland had longed for a hero with Bobby's good looks, power and speed. Tom Tenda could hit, of course, but he never had the handsome face and the teen-age appeal that were so much a part of Bobby Reynolds. And for all Tom's power and skill, he had never hit a baseball 550 feet in his life.

Advance ticket sales had been very good. Bobby was a big drawing card but now the fans, who were growing tired of waiting, began calling for him to bang out some home runs.

"I'm worried," Alexander said to Speed Peters when the club came home from Chicago. "We have built up the boy and the fans are expecting a lot. If he doesn't come through soon, they are going to begin booing him. And if they do that, they may never stop, no matter how good he becomes. It happened to Mays and Mantle in New York. It could happen here to Reynolds."

Sox Park was filled the following night for the game against the Bengals. The two teams had been bitter rivals for years and enjoyed beating each other out of pennants. Even when one team was in last place, it could be counted on to rise up against the other. Down through the years, the Bengal-Sox contest had been equaled only by the competition between the old Brooklyn Dodgers and the New York Giants.

This year, the Sox and the Bengals were rated as the ones to beat for the pennant. The experts agreed that only the Bombers had a chance to edge them out.

"A victory now," Yank told the Sox, "is just as important as a victory the last day of the season."

"You can say that again," Tenda shouted, looking at Jennings. "Let's get out there and win."

The Sox ran up the dugout steps, exploding full

of fight onto the freshly cut grass of the ball field.

"Big one today," Louie shouted. "We win a big one today."

Lester Watt, a lefthander, built like a barrel, who had won 20 games for three straight years, started for the Bengals. Saltin was the Sox pitcher. Bobby was in rightfield, batting seventh. "I get one today," Bobby promised himself. "An important one."

In the eighth inning Bobby had his chance. The Bengals were leading, 2–0, when Sunderlin sliced a two-out single to left. Groten banged a double to center, sending Sunderlin to third.

Bobby stood up in the on-deck circle and dug his right toe into the dirt. He walked up to the plate

slowly, determined to hit at least a single to tie the game, and hoping to hit a home run to put the Sox ahead. The fans exploded into wild cheering, begging him to hit one as far as the papers said he could.

"Come on, big boy," someone yelled. "Hit one like the Babe!"

Bobby planted his feet firmly and lifted his bat high. Watt's first pitch cut the outside corner and Bobby did not move his bat.

"Strike one," the umpire behind the plate said.

The next pitch came in toward the heart of the plate and broke sharply over the inside corner. Bobby swung hard and missed. Bengal catcher Tim Abernathy held the ball under Bobby's nose.

"That is what is called a curve ball, son," Tim said. "You are no big leaguer until you learn how to hit them."

Bobby knew that when a pitcher has two strikes and no balls on a batter, he uses an old baseball trick. He throws what is known as a waste pitch. The ball is never intended to come across for a strike. It is supposed to come just close enough to get an over-eager batter to swing.

Watt, who lived by the book, threw a waste pitch. But Bobby, in the excitement of the moment, forgot what he had learned. Instead, he swung hard and his bat fanned the air. He had missed the ball by half a foot.

"That's your third strike out today, you bonus bum," a fan yelled.

"What a waste of $60,000," shouted another.

As if on signal, most of the Sox fans began their booing. They continued until Bobby was back in rightfield, where he wanted nothing more than to dig a hole and crawl in.

A few lines in the morning newspaper told how everyone seemed to feel. Under Bobby's picture were the words: "The $60,000 Bonus Bust!"

chapter 7

PEP TALK FROM AN OLD PRO

"Bonus bust" is one of the most stinging remarks in baseball. Bobby had been reading about bonus busts since he was 12. But he had never known how deeply the words could cut into a player's pride, or weaken his confidence. He found out when he read the Sunday *Gazette*.

In a full-page story in the *Gazette*, Marvin Gillette reminded his readers of the big bonus busts of the past. He wrote about Paul Pettit, the pitcher who had received a $100,000 bonus and paid back the Pittsburgh Pirates with only one big-league victory. He wrote about Bruce Swango, who had taken $36,000 from the Baltimore Orioles before he found out that he became nervous while pitching before

80

big crowds. He wrote about the $25,000 that the Brooklyn Dodgers had handed Danny Lynk, a short-stop who could play a ukelele, but couldn't even hit in the minor leagues.

Marv summed up by writing: "A large amount of cash has been lost by ball clubs who gave out big money to players with little talent. It would not sur-prise me one bit if the Sox have thrown away $60,000. Bobby Reynolds seems to be one of the biggest bonus busts of all time. The way Reynolds has been playing, the money he took for signing makes him seem like the biggest robber since Jesse James ran wild in the Old West."

Charlie Lewis read Gillette's story and threw the *Gazette* on the floor. "Don't you believe it, Bobby," he said. "That Gillette is the worst trouble maker in the newspaper business."

Bobby was sitting in a large chair. He fought back the tears. "I don't know," he said. "I don't know. Maybe he is right. I can't hit. I am hurting the team. I really haven't earned a penny of my money."

Charlie paced up and down on the carpet. He tried to think of something comforting to say, but he was unable to come up with the right words. There was a sharp knock. Charlie opened the door. Lard Jennings stood there, his 200 pounds filling the entrance.

"Hi, Lard," Charlie said. "Glad to see you. Come

on in." Charlie looked surprised at the big man's call.

"Hello, Charlie. Hello, Bobby."

Reynolds looked up. "Hello, Lard," he said slowly.

"I was near here," Lard said, "and I thought I would drop in for a visit. You boys mind if I stay awhile?"

"Not at all, Lard," Charlie said. "Glad to have you."

The big pitcher took off his sport jacket and placed it carefully on a chair. He rolled up the sleeves of his gray, open-collar shirt and dropped with a thump into the blue sofa. Then he winked at Charlie. "Charlie," he said, "I thought I saw a friend of yours waiting for you in the lobby."

Charlie scratched his head. Then he smiled, picking up the hint. "Sure, Lard," he said, "an old Army buddy of mine. I was supposed to meet him today. Thought I told him to come on up, but I guess I said I would meet him downstairs. Thanks a lot. I had better get going."

Charlie walked to the closet, took out a jacket, put it over his arm and hurried out the door. He was happy that the wise old pro was taking over the job of cheering up the bonus kid.

Lard leaned back and lit a big cigar. With smoke rings circling over his head, he began to speak. "Bobby, my boy," Lard said, "have you read the

papers this morning, I mean the sports page?"

"Just the *Gazette*."

"Exactly the paper I had in mind. Marv Gillette is a pretty good writer, don't you think?"

"I guess so."

"Sometimes what Marvin writes hurts pretty badly."

Bobby looked up at the ceiling, tears beginning to fill his blue eyes. "You can say that again."

"I will say that again. Sometimes what Marvin writes hurts pretty badly. And sometimes what Marvin writes is not the truth. Like today!"

"What do you mean he does not write the truth?"

"I mean that right now you are probably saying to yourself that you haven't done anything to help the club and haven't been earning a penny of the money you got, and maybe you are a robber as Gillette says."

"Right," Bobby said. "That is exactly what I have been saying, and it seems as though I am right."

"Right! Right!" Lard was on his feet, fire in his eyes. "That is the most wrong thing I have ever heard in my life."

"What do you mean?" Bobby said.

Jennings sat down, stretching his long legs in front of him. "When I broke into baseball 16 years ago," he said, "I signed a contract for peanuts. And I mean peanuts. They were paying almost nothing in the minor leagues. I had a wife and a kid and I worked as a carpenter during the off season to make ends meet.

"Finally the Sox brought me up and I stuck with them. My rookie year in the big leagues I made almost nothing. I started to win some ball games and I began to get raises and seven years ago, when I won 27 games and a pennant for them, I was rewarded with a big contract.

"They paid me well while I was winning, but when my fast ball began to go, my pay was cut."

"But you have money in the bank," Bobby said.

"Sure, I have money in the bank, but not as much as you think. I have had to support my wife and three kids and live the way people expect a big-league star to live. That costs money. It means good clothes and good tips and a car. It means expensive restaurants. It means picking up checks for your friends, and a lot of other things. If I told you how little money I have in the bank, you would be surprised."

"Don't you make money between seasons?"

"A little bit and only recently. Two years ago I put some money into a bowling alley. But before that, I would go on the road with an All-Star team for a month, and then go home. I wasn't trained for any kind of work and no one had any good ideas for me. They all figured that a big star had all the money he needed.

"I couldn't even do manual labor after I made it in the big leagues. If I had, everybody would have talked about me behind my back. So I didn't do anything from the end of the road trips to the beginning of the season. All I did was spend."

"I never realized that," Bobby said.

"No, I'm sure you didn't. I don't think too many people do realize it. Now, I'm not telling you this because I want you to feel sorry for me. All in all, baseball has been pretty good to me. But I just want to show you another side of this game.

"When I was pitching in spring training, I was

fighting for my job. Every game I had ever won before meant nothing. I had to prove all over again that I wasn't washed up. The day Yank feels that I can't help this club, I am finished. No hanging on because I won 191 games. Just goodby, see you around."

Lard stood up and walked to the window. "Bobby, what do you know about Babe Ruth?" he said.

"I know a lot about Babe Ruth," Bobby said. "My dad used to tell me stories about him all the time."

"He used to tell you stories about home runs, and big crowds, and a lot of cheering, right?"

"Yes, he did."

"Well, I want to tell you another story about Babe Ruth. About what happened to him when the home runs weren't coming and when the big cheers were dying down. It happened in 1935, eight years after the Babe hit those 60 home runs in one season.

"Babe was 39 then and his power was gone. The Yankees had been paying him a big salary and they decided he wasn't worth it any more. So they released him—to the Boston Braves. No hanging around because of all of his wins. Goodby, Babe. Thanks for the pennants you won for us, and thanks for the millions of dollars you made for us. See you around, fellow.

"You know, Bobby, a lot of guys say that the Babe began to die a little as soon as he left the Yankees. He had said all along that when he was

86

through playing for the Yankees, he wanted to be a coach or a manager for them. But they never gave him a chance. And the Braves didn't do much for him either. Before the year was up, they told the Babe to hand in his uniform. The only job they were willing to give him was in sales promotion. They wanted him to go around making speeches and selling tickets. Of course, the Babe turned them down."

"I never knew that," Bobby said. "I never knew anything about that."

"Look, Bobby, the point of all this is that baseball is a business, a business the same as selling stocks or running a grocery store or sitting at a typewriter.

"Suppose a big business man puts $60,000 in a steel company, Bobby. What do you think he is putting the money in for?"

"To make more money," Bobby said.

"Right. And what happens if the company fails? Does the owner of the steel mill ever think of giving back the money, or does he ever think of himself as a robber?"

"No," Bobby said. "Not if it was a fair and square deal."

"Right. Now you made a fair and square deal with the Sox. You took a $60,000 contract to play baseball. If you succeed, then it is a good deal, and that is all there is to it. As long as you try your best, you are no robber or anything like it.

"And let's suppose you don't make good. If the Sox release you, they have to pay you the full $60,000. You are guaranteed that, right?"

"That's right," Bobby said. "If I stay in baseball, they pay me the $60,000 spread out in salary over five years. But I am guaranteed the $60,000. I get it all if they release me. I don't get it if I quit. But if they let me go, I have to get all the money."

"Okay," Lard said. "So if you don't make good, you have $60,000 and you go to college and you use the rest of the money to set yourself up in a business. All that will mean is that you have made money out of baseball. You are making the score even with baseball for the profit they have made on guys like me and guys like the Babe."

Bobby's face lit up. "But I want to make good anyway," he said.

"Bobby," Lard said, "of course you do. All I was doing was showing you the worst possible picture. I have been around for a long time and seen a lot of young ball players. I know talent when I see it, and you have talent. I know that before long you are going to be worth ten times that $60,000 to the Sox."

chapter 8

FOUR UP AND FOUR OUT

Bobby was bursting with excitement. His giant steps carried him to the entrance of the ball park before Lard had even slammed the cab door.

"Come on, Lard," Bobby said. "Let's go."

The big pitcher grunted and walked toward the dressing room. "Slow down, Bobby," he said. "Easy, easy."

"It's your own fault," Bobby said. His blue eyes were bright. "Your pep talk did it. I want to get my hands on a bat."

Bobby couldn't wait any longer. He ran the last few steps to his locker. Sunderlin looked up in surprise.

"Look at the Golden Boy," the shortstop said.

"You would think someone had given him another $60,000."

Bobby paid no attention. They could kid him all they wanted. He didn't care. He just wanted to hit the ball. He jammed his gray jacket onto a hook and pulled his red polo shirt over his head. He kicked off his shoes and reached for his spikes. Then he felt a strong arm dragging him away. It belonged to Charlie Lewis.

"Don't miss this," Charlie said. "Louie and Saltin are at it again."

Charlie and Bobby elbowed in among the players surrounding the rubbing table.

Saltin lay on the table, his right arm wrapped in hot towels. "To recapitulate," he said, "I think we are going to run away with this pennant once our hitting picks up."

Ziller scratched his head. "To re-what?"

"To recapitulate, Louie. That means to review briefly. To sum up."

Surprisingly, Louie's pleasant features changed. "You think you are pretty smart, don't you? Always using those big words."

"To tell you the truth, I never think about them."

"Oh, yeah? Well, I know some big words, too."

"Really, Louie?"

"Really. You want to hear one?"

The coach's helper removed the towels and began

rubbing the muscles in Saltin's arm. Roger gritted his teeth in pain. "I would be honored to hear one, Louie," he said.

"Okay," Louie said, smiling. "Delicatessen." He let the word sink in. "That big enough?"

The Sox roared. "You scored that time, Louie," Sunderlin said.

Regan stroked the air with his finger, as if he were making a mark on a blackboard. "Score one for Ziller," he said. "Ziller leads, 1–0."

O'Connor's booming voice broke up the session. "Batting practice in ten minutes. Everybody out in ten minutes."

Batting practice began with a bang. The first time one of the Sox hit the ball, a small man in the stands banged a big bass drum. Groups of fans were already filling the stands. Sunday double-headers draw the real fans. They come out early, dressed in sport shirts and slacks and loaded with sandwiches. They stay at the park until the last man is out, rooting until the last ball is thrown.

Bobby chased fly balls in the outfield, then raced in to hit. Regan was at the plate, hitting low line drives past the scrambling infielders.

"He's only a singles hitter," a fan called. "Get him out of there! Let's see some big hitters! Let's see Big Tom hit."

Regan hit another line drive and shot a stream of

tobacco juice through his teeth. He stepped out of the batting cage.

"A big hitter," the fan called again. "Get Tenda up there."

"Reynolds," another fan yelled. "Let's see the Golden Boy hit."

Bobby twisted his ring and picked up three bats. He swung them around his head and threw two to the ground. He dug his right toe into the ground and pushed himself toward the cage. Inside, he planted his feet firmly and stared at the rightfield fence.

The rightfield fence in Sox Park measures 320 feet down the foul line. It swings in a wide curve toward centerfield and at its deepest point in right center is 460 feet from home plate. A bright red sign

marks the 460-foot spot, and only a few men have ever hit the ball over the sign.

Bobby nodded to batting-practice pitcher Sam Beaumont. Sam swung into an easy windup and threw a curve to the outside corner. Swinging with the pitch, Bobby placed a perfect line-drive single to leftfield.

Beaumont followed with a fast ball, waist high and inside. Bobby swung gracefully and smacked the ball hard. The moment the ball left his bat, the fans howled. It rose swiftly, hugging the rightfield line and went over the fence.

Bobby swung again and caught a high fast ball with all of his power. The ball sped toward right centerfield. It flew over the red 460-foot sign, bringing the fans to their feet.

"Again," they yelled. "Again!" This was what they had been waiting for.

Three more times, Bobby banged the ball over the fence. The fellows in the stands pounded each other on the back. They were sure they had the pennant. The bonus kid was going to win it for them. See, he wasn't a flop, after all.

"Good hitting, kid," Coach Templeton said, as Bobby ran toward the dugout.

Regan stood at the water fountain frowning. "Wait and see what he does in the ball game."

By the time the first game began, more than

40,000 fans were jammed into Sox Park. They waved white score cards. They jumped up and down. They spilled soda and they smeared themselves, as well as their hot dogs, with mustard. They wanted to root the Sox home all the way.

In the first inning, Tenda banged a triple with two men on base to put the Sox ahead, 2–0. With two out in the fourth, the Bombers got three hits, scoring one run. They had runners on second and third when Johnny Lombardi, their big hitter, came to the plate.

Phil Robinson stood on the mound, sweat dripping down his face. He leaned toward the plate to pick out catcher Tenda's signal. He wound up and twisted a curve over the outside corner. Lombardi swung from his heels and missed.

"Good work," Charlie yelled from second base.

"Swinging at air, honey," shortstop Sunderlin called. "Way to pitch, Phil, baby."

Lombardi's big muscles rippled. He kicked the dirt in the batter's box and got set to hit. His jaw was set, his eyes were fastened on the pitcher.

Robinson's second curve ball hung for a split second as it came up to the plate. Before the ball broke, Lombardi lashed it down the third-base line, a sure single, probably a double.

The ball skimmed over the far corner of the bag and Ziller, diving, scooped it out of the dirt. Louie

was on the ground, in no position to throw to first. There was only one play he could make. Louie slid forward, scraping his stomach, and tagged the Bomber runner as he barreled into third.

Sunderlin helped Louie up. "You saved us, Louie," he said. "You sure did save us. That was a beautiful play."

In the bottom of the seventh inning, with the score still 2–1, Bobby had a chance to break up the ball game. He came up with the bases loaded and one man out and he smashed the ball hard. But it whistled straight at the shortstop, who turned it into a double play.

"Tough break," Charlie said. "But you belted it good. Keep it up."

The Sox hung on and won, 2–1. They mobbed Robinson at the mound and trooped to the locker room for a brief, but happy, rest.

Between games, the players took off their wet sweat shirts and pulled on clean ones. They drank sodas in single gulps and talked noisily.

"Louie, my boy," Saltin said. "You were great. Great, great, great."

Ziller grinned from ear to ear. "Now there is a word I understand," he said.

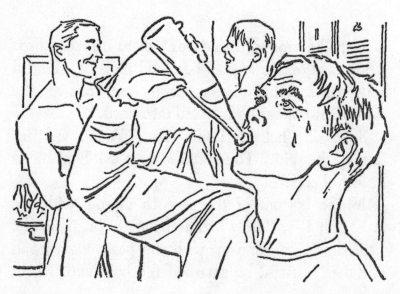

Bobby hadn't made a hit, but he was happy. He always tried to remember that team success was more important than personal glory. "Maybe in the second game I'll get the hits," he said to himself.

Yank O'Connor was smiling, too. "Same lineup," he said, "except for the pitcher. York pitches the second game."

Bill York, a lean lefthander, was a strange pitcher. When Bill's control was sharp, nobody could hit his blazing fast ball. But when Bill was wild, he gave up his speed and tried to aim the ball. On those days, he generally ended up taking an early shower.

This was one of York's wild days. He walked the first two men. Then, with Lombardi at bat, Bill tried to aim a pitch over the plate. The Bombers' big first baseman waited as the ball floated up to him. Finally, he let go his swing. His bat met the ball with a loud thump. The ball was in the stands for a three-run homer.

Yank O'Connor kicked up dust as he moved to the mound. He waved for a new pitcher and took the ball away from York.

"But, Yank, I'm pitching okay," York said. "I just haven't had any luck."

Yank flipped the ball in the air and caught it. "I know that, son," he said. "But let's see if I can't get a pitcher in here who will have a little luck."

O'Connor brought in Rabbit Nestor, a right

hander with a sweeping curve ball and what the ball players call "a load of pitching savvy." Rabbit did not try to fire the ball past the hitters. He simply tried to fool them. He usually succeeded.

Rabbit pitched perfectly for four innings. So did Ernie Russo, the Bombers' pitcher. In the fifth, first-baseman Red Castigan doubled to the left for the first Sox hit. Bobby walked up to the plate, tapping his bat in time to the hand clapping of the fans.

The hands in the ball park thundered together. The voices called out in time. "We—want—a—hit." Clap—clap—clap—clap.

"Just like in batting practice," a fellow yelled.

"Another one over the 460-foot sign."

"A big one, Bobby. A big one."

Bobby twisted his body into a furious swing. He belted the ball down the rightfield line and over the fence. The fans' roar faded into a groan. The ball was foul.

The next pitch cut the inside corner for strike two. Russo wasted one outside and Bobby held up his swing. On his third pitch, Ernie drew back and whipped forward with his big motion. Bobby expected a fast ball and brought his bat around in a hard, level swing. But the pitch was a change-up. He swung at air for strike three. The next two Sox batters were thrown out at first.

Lard Jennings came in to pitch in the seventh

inning. The old-timer's knuckle ball puzzled the Bombers for three innings and the fans roared with delight. Few men in Sox history had been more popular than Lard. The fans cheered him on when he stuffed his glove in his back pocket and walked to the bench in the ninth.

"Attaboy, Lard," they shouted. "We'll get those runs back. We'll get your first win."

Tenda peeled off his catcher's equipment and grabbed two bats from the dugout rack. He walked with confidence to home plate.

"Come on, Tom," Templeton yelled.

Tenda nodded and dumped a curve ball into left-field. Before the shouting had a chance to die down, Sunderlin whistled a sharp single to right and Saltin walked.

The Bomber manager, Teddy Jensen, ran to the mound, stuck his face an inch away from Russo's and bellowed at him.

"You tired?" Jensen said. "You losing your stuff? Don't lie to me! Tell me!"

"No," Russo said. "No. I'm okay."

"One more hit," Jensen said. "One more hit and it's the ball game for you."

The manager walked slowly off the field and Regan went up to the plate. Russo threw a slow ball that seemed to coast toward Regan. Regan swung and the ball rose high in the air, falling back of second base. A hit, but not deep enough to bring in more than one runner. Tenda came running in from third base. Three–one, and the bases still loaded with no outs.

Jensen, the Bomber manager, took Russo out and replaced him with Jim Moore, his best relief pitcher. Moore threw a few practice pitches and then watched as Charlie Lewis walked to the plate. Moore let loose a fast ball that zoomed in toward the inside of home plate. Charlie swung, hitting a slow roller toward the Bombers' third baseman, who ran forward to scoop it up. But he couldn't get his hands on the ball. He fumbled it. An error! Sunderlin raced home and Charlie was safe on first. The score was 3–2. The stands went wild!

Ziller and Castigan hit grounders, easy outs, and the stands grew still as Bobby came to bat.

"Now, big boy," they shouted. "Now. Hit it a mile. Hit it like this morning."

Bobby swung at the first pitch and lifted a lazy pop-up almost straight up in the air. Moore smothered it in his glove. It was over quickly.

"Four times up and four times out," Bobby said.

He sat in the club house for a long time after the game, the words of a loud, angry fan ringing in his ears. "You bum," the fan had yelled. "Showing off this morning doesn't mean a thing. They only count in the ball game."

chapter 9

A DAY OF REST

The right words refused to come. Bobby sat at his desk, holding his pen. He was writing a letter to his dad. He wanted to write something cheerful, but he couldn't. "All my letters home are the same," he thought. "All about my troubles. I bet Mom and Dad are really worried."

Bobby tugged at his shirt collar, stared at the paper. He had written half a page. He wanted to write more, but he could not think straight. He thought he heard someone whistling hard. Funny, how your mind can play tricks on you when it is mixed up with so many confusing thoughts. Wait a second. Someone *was* whistling. At the door.

Bobby ran to the door and opened it. Tony was

standing there. Tony was the friend he had met during spring training. Tony was back from the minor leagues. Bobby yelled for Charlie. "Charlie, hey, Charlie! Tony's here. Tony is back."

Bobby grinned from ear to ear. He wanted to know all about it. He pulled Tony into the living room. He shot out questions without waiting for answers.

Tony put his fingers between his lips and split the air with another sharp whistle. "Easy, Bobby," he said. "Slow down. One question at a time."

"It's great," Bobby said. "Just great. When did they let you know? When did they bring you back?"

"Yesterday. Mr. Alexander called me and said to get on a plane. The Sox just traded Sunderlin, he told me. You are back in the big leagues, he said. We need you to play shortstop."

"Move in with us," Bobby said. "We have room. We have a lot of room. Right, Charlie?"

"Sure, we have room," Charlie said. "The three rookie wildcats, that's what we will be. We are going to rip this league apart."

Tony whistled. "Right apart. That's just what we will do," he said. "Rip this league right apart."

Bobby's face dropped. "You guys will," he said, "but not me. Not the way I'm going. Tony, you should have seen me yesterday. Rapped the ball all over the park in practice and did nothing in the game. Hits in practice don't count, Tony."

"You'll get going," Tony said. "We will tear this league apart. All three of us. I'll whistle until you swing easy or until you think there is a locomotive loose in your head." He put his fingers to his lips and let loose another ear-splitting whistle.

"Let's forget baseball today," Charlie said. "There's no ball game and we should try to forget it. How about going somewhere?"

"Right," Tony said. "We can celebrate my return to the Sox."

"We can go to a fancy restaurant and eat dinner," Charlie said.

"And then how about going to hear the band at the dance hall?" Bobby said.

"Great! Great!" said Tony. "Let me take the clothes out of my suitcase and then we will get going. Little Tony Luco is back in the big leagues— for keeps." He threw one arm around Charlie and the other around Bobby.

Tony whistled. "Get in line," he yelled. "Behind me."

The three boys lined up one behind the other, Tony in front, Charlie in the middle, and Bobby, who towered over both of them, behind.

"Repeat after me," Tony said. "We are going to tear this league apart."

Tony marched toward the bedroom, Charlie and Bobby behind him. They marched and they sang, like cheer leaders at a game. Finally, they fell to the floor in a three-man heap, laughing.

They got up and Tony ran to his suitcase. He flipped it on the couch and began to toss his clothes into drawers. Suddenly, he spotted a thick, green book on the coffee table.

"Boy, that book takes up a lot of room," he said. "What is it?"

Tony reached down and lifted the book. He pretended that the weight was too much for him. "English literature," he said. "No wonder I can hardly hold it up. Pretty heavy reading. Whose book is it?"

"Mine," Bobby said. "Roger Saltin gave it to me." "Why?"

"He thinks I should go to college when I'm not playing ball. Says this will help me get started."

"Learning anything from it?" Tony said.

"I learned one thing right away," Bobby said. "I learned that Herodotus was an ancient Greek, not a third baseman for the old Yankees, the way Louie Ziller said."

Tony whistled. "Louie Ziller is great," he said. "Good old Louie."

"Roger Saltin has been great, too," Bobby said. "He and Lard and Louie are about the only older ones who are talking to me. Roger has made me want to go to college, too. I sent away to three schools for information. You know, school catalogues."

Charlie smiled. "You know what we do, Tony?" he said. "We do what Louie does with Roger. We let Bobby pay and then we learn all his knowledge for nothing." Charlie wrinkled his nose and spoke in a high-pitched voice, like Ziller's. Everybody laughed.

"Let's get a move on," Bobby said. "I'm starved."

A while later, the three boys sat in Romero's restaurant. They sank into the soft velvet seats, staring at the crystal lights and the well-dressed people. Many of the men wore dinner jackets, and the women gowns and furs. The three felt out of place.

A waiter bowed and asked for their orders.

"The three biggest steaks in the house," Bobby said. He turned to Tony. "That's the way Lard Jennings does it. Real class, huh?"

Before the steaks arrived, a waiter had filled the bread basket on their table with three orders of biscuits. "You boys certainly can eat," he said.

At eight o'clock, the three Sox arrived at the dance hall. "Great band tonight," Bobby said. "Modern Jazz Quartet, Chris Connor and Miles Davis."

"Miles Davis?" Tony said. "Doesn't he pitch for the Bombers?"

"No, you clown," Bobby said. "Do you want to sound like Louie?"

"What's the matter with you, Tony?" Charlie said. "Everybody knows that Miles Davis is the Bengal catcher."

Bobby grabbed Tony's head with one hand and Charlie's with the other. He knocked them together lightly. "You are nuts," he said, laughing. "Miles Davis plays trumpet."

The boys bought seats in the second row and walked to them in a single line. "We are going to rip this league apart," Tony said. He turned to the others and asked them to join in. Bobby's long arm reached over Charlie's head and slapped Tony.

"Not here," he said, a big grin spreading across his face.

The boys settled in their seats just as the music

began. Davis' trumpet brought the crowd to its feet. Bobby's fingers drummed, keeping time with the music. "Wish I could play like that," he whispered.

When Chris Connor came on stage, Charlie sat up straight in his seat. "I like the singers," he said. "I'm not much for that instrument music."

Chris began singing in her deep voice. Charlie stared at her. "About time you shut up," Bobby said, poking him in the ribs.

When the Modern Jazz Quartet walked on stage, Charlie began to grin. "Get a load of the beards," he said. "What do you say? Let's grow beards."

"Great idea," Bobby said. "We could really shake up old Yank."

"Can you see it?" Tony said. "Can you just see Yank blowing his stack?"

"Can you see Louie?" Bobby said, in a squeaky voice like Ziller's.

Bobby twisted in his seat, laughing. He felt a piece of paper in his shirt pocket. He reached into the pocket and pulled out the paper. It was the letter to his dad that he had not finished. "I can finish this later," he said to himself.

Bobby had no way of knowing that his dad was in the Sox offices at that very moment, talking with Yank O'Connor.

Yank and Bobby's dad were in the manager's office. Yank was sitting in the armchair behind his desk. Mr. Reynolds was sitting up straight on the leather sofa.

"I didn't want to come," Mr. Reynolds was saying. "I didn't want to come, but I had to. I don't want Bobby to know I am here. All of his letters home have been sad ones. He says nothing is going right. He can't hit, he can't make friends. Mr. O'Connor, Bobby is 18 years old. He is only a boy. This could hurt him."

He began again. "What I'm trying to say, Mr. O'Connor, is that I think Bobby will never be a success if he stays here any longer. I think you should send him back to Oakmont for another season. He will hit there. Don't hurt him. Give him another year in the minors."

Yank O'Connor looked up at the ceiling. Then he turned to Bobby's father. "Mr. Reynolds," he said, "I might go ahead and do just that."

chapter 10

THE GOODBY BLAST

Yank O'Connor sat in the wooden armchair without moving, and stared straight into Bobby's eyes. The bonus kid wrapped his fingers around his ring. He turned it until it pinched with pain.

Yank's booming voice broke the silence. "Take it easy," he said. "All your troubles are over."

"What do you mean?"

"You are going to Oakmont, Bobby. Turn in your uniform after today's game. You can pick up your airplane ticket here tomorrow morning."

Now that it had happened, Bobby couldn't believe it. He wanted to argue with the manager. He wanted to tell Yank that he needed another chance. But he knew better. Bobby had learned that lesson.

"I'm running this ball club," Yank had told him.

Bobby did not want to talk back. All he could say was "Oakmont?"

O'Connor frowned. He was tired. His wrinkles seemed to cover his entire face. "Yes, Bobby, Oakmont. And you're going to hit there, just as you did last year. Pretty soon you will realize how silly all of this was. You will realize that the only reason you didn't hit in the big leagues was because you tried too hard. When you come back, Bobby, you will be able to stay right on top with our best players."

The manager stood up and extended his heavy arm. His hand trembled slightly. "So long for now."

Bobby walked out of the office and went slowly toward the locker room. He pulled his uniform from the hook in his locker and stared at the number 14. "They will put you away," he thought. "But I will be wearing you next year. One more game and then you get a long rest."

The locker room was quiet. All of the other players were on the field, taking batting practice. Bobby dressed slowly. "No sense rushing," he thought. "Nothing matters here any more. I am going to Oakmont. I don't know, maybe it won't be the worst thing in the world. It was not so bad last year. At least they like me there."

"Hey, Reynolds! You coming out today or you going to sleep in the locker room?"

It was Coach Templeton, and he looked burned up. "Coming right out, Billy. What's the hurry?"

"What's the hurry? The game is almost ready to begin. That's the hurry."

"So what? I'm through."

"Not until tomorrow. Now you are in the starting lineup."

"How come?"

"I think the old man wants you to hit one home run before you go. Go ahead, do it for him."

Bobby tied the laces on his spiked shoes and ran up the runway onto the field. He caught up with the Sox as they ran to their positions.

"Where you been?" Regan said, "We should have sent a taxi to drive you to rightfield."

In the third inning, Bobby walked to the plate. He smiled as the fans began to boo him. "Get all the booing done today," he said to himself. "You will have to go to California to boo me tomorrow."

Bobby settled into the batter's box. He held his bat high and gripped the handle loosely. Tony whistled. "You don't have to whistle," Bobby thought. "I'm swinging easy today."

Sid Harker looked around the field to make sure all the Bombers were in position. Then, he fired a fast ball, high and inside. Bobby lashed his bat in a smooth, level swing and the ball took off. It shot high over the first baseman's head and sped toward

rightfield. The rightfielder never moved. He simply
turned around and watched the baseball soar over
the fence.

Tony and Charlie ran to home plate to greet the
bonus kid. "That's the way to do it, boy! What a
beautiful hit!"

Yank O'Connor stumbled over a bat as he walked
to the water fountain. As the water ran into his mouth,
he smiled. Then he stood up, forced a frown, and
glared at the bonus kid.

The next time he was at bat, Bobby hit a double
down the rightfield line.

"Atta boy," a fan yelled. "Now you are hitting
them when they count."

"Sounds like the same guy who yelled at me Sunday," Bobby thought.

In the eighth inning, the Sox came up trailing, 3–1. Bobby's homer had given them their only run. The fans filled the air with cheers. "We want a hit —we want a hit." Clap—clap—clap—clap.

Tony led off with a single. Castigan walked. Bobby leaped out of the on-deck circle and almost ran up to the plate. "Now to give them one to remember me by," he whispered. "Here comes the goodby blast."

The fans clapped their hands in rhythm. "Now, big boy," they yelled. "Hit one now."

Harker turned and faked a throw to second. Tony dove head first and grabbed the bag with his fingers. He stood up, brushed off the dirt and whistled. "Here I go, pitcher, look at me. I'm stealing. Watch me! Watch me!"

Bobby waved his bat back and forth. "Tony really is rattling him," he thought. "Harker might forget me. He might put one right down the middle. Keep it up, Tony. Shake him. Rattle him."

Castigan edged off first. He picked up Tony's cry. "I'm going, too," Castigan yelled. "Double steal. Double steal."

Harker tried not to listen to the runners. He put his foot on the rubber, then whirled toward second and began to throw. Suddenly he held up his throw.

Neither shortstop nor second baseman was covering!

At once the Sox bench and the stands stood up. "Balk," everybody yelled.

Harker's foot had been on the rubber when he turned. According to the rules, he had to throw the ball to the batter. Since he had not thrown, the runners were allowed to move up one base each. Manager Teddy Jensen flew from the Bomber dugout. "What's the matter with you?" he said to Harker.

"I thought they were stealing. I wanted to pick off Luco."

"Forget the base runners. Just pitch. This kid is a sucker for an outside curve. Throw him one."

Bobby continued to pump his bat, back and forth, back and forth. Harker wound up and twisted an outside curve. Bobby waited for it to break. He took his time and swung with that smooth, level motion. He put the full power of his 220 pounds into the swing and the smack of bat upon ball sounded all through the ball park.

The bonus kid took three steps down the first-base line, then he leaped into the air. The ball was flying over the 460-foot sign.

He ran around the bases, a big grin on his face. "I hit one for the old man," he said as he passed Templeton at third base. "I did it for him."

"You sure did," Templeton said.

After the game, Lard Jennings pounded Bobby on the back. "Now you are on your way," Lard said. "Good game."

"I sure am on my way," Bobby thought. "On my way to Oakmont."

Off in a corner, Regan shot a stream of tobacco juice to the ground. "About time he did something," Regan said.

Tenda wrapped a towel around his waist and took a bar of soap from the top shelf of his locker. "Yeah, it sure is about time," he said. "I want to see him keep it up. That's what I want to see."

Bobby began to pull off his uniform. "I'm just like my little dog back home," he thought, as he threw his spikes on the concrete. "Funny little dog. We tried to teach him how to roll over. We would hold up a bone and say, 'Over, over.' He would try but he couldn't do it. Fell all over himself, he wanted that bone so badly. Funniest thing, though, was later when I looked into the back yard. No bone, nobody around and that silly dog was rolling over."

Templeton walked over. "Yank says you should be here tomorrow," the coach said. "We will have your ticket for you then."

Tony and Charlie dressed quickly and waited for Bobby. "Big night tonight," Tony said when they walked out of the ball park. "We are going to celebrate your two home runs."

"Rare steaks and everything," Charlie said.

"Sounds good," Bobby said. He draped his arms around his friends. "But we celebrate more than the home runs."

"What else?" Tony said.

"We celebrate my last day with the Sox. I'm going to Oakmont tomorrow."

"What?" Charlie and Tony said.

"Just what I said. O'Connor told me this afternoon. The last homer was my goodby blast."

chapter 11

THE BONUS KID GROWS UP

Bobby was surrounded. The kids came tumbling over the fences. They popped out from between parked cars. They touched his clothes, they pounded him on the back. They called his name.

"Bobby Reynolds, Bobby Reynolds."

"Sign this, Bobby Reynolds."

Score cards, pieces of paper, magazines were held out to him. Bobby grinned and pushed his pencil quickly.

"Sign under your picture."

"Sign it to Jimmy."

He was a hero in the big leagues. What if it was only for a day! It felt great. These kids did not know he was leaving for Oakmont in the morning.

"I'll sign for everybody," Bobby said.

The next morning Bobby packed his suitcases. He said goodby to Tony and Charlie. "I have to get out to the park early," he said. "I guess I won't see you guys until next year. You two can tear the league apart this year, and next year we will tear it apart together."

When Bobby walked into the dressing room, Templeton rushed up to him. "You're not going for another day," the coach said. "We couldn't get you on a plane. You play today, and you leave tomorrow."

Suddenly, it hit Bobby. He wasn't going to Oakmont. Yank never intended to send him to Oakmont. They could not fool him any more.

Bobby threw his jacket into the locker and rushed to O'Connor's small office. Without knocking on the door, Bobby walked in and planted himself in the armchair.

Five minutes later, Yank walked in. He looked at Bobby and laughed. "You taking over this ball club, Bobby?" he said. "What are you doing in my chair?"

Bobby bounced to his feet. He took two steps toward the manager and glared at him. "You can't fool me, Yank," he said. "I know what you are doing."

O'Connor stared straight at him. "You do?"

"Yes. You plan to keep me on a string. Every day,

you are going to make up an excuse for keeping me here. That way, I'll be loose up at the plate. I won't worry about striking out. I will just go up and swing away." Bobby made the statement and then looked hard at Yank to see how he was taking it.

Yank slipped past Bobby and sat on the edge of his desk. "You figured it out, all right," he said. "Smart boy." The manager laughed, a long, low laugh. Bobby laughed, too.

"You never intended to send me to Oakmont," Bobby said again.

"No, I didn't," Yank said. He laughed again.

"Well, it worked yesterday," Bobby said. "It worked yesterday and it is going to work today. And all season long. I don't care what anyone says. I'm going to swing easy. Nothing is going to rattle me.

I'm not going to let you down. It worked yesterday. It is going to work all season."

Yank slapped Bobby's arm. "That is the way, Bobby," he said. "Just swing easy and take your time up there. Don't listen to the fans. Don't listen to the wise guys on the team. Shut them up with your bat."

Bobby ran out of the office. He grabbed Tony and Charlie. He dragged them to the center of the locker room floor. "I'm not going to Oakmont," he said. "I am staying right here. I can hit in the big leagues. You saw it yesterday."

Bobby whirled around and faced the corner where Regan, Gordon and Tenda were dressing. "I'm going to stay here all season," he said, "whether the guys on the ball club like it or not."

Bobby walked to the plate in the third inning that afternoon with two men on base. He smiled as he heard Tony's sharp whistle. He pumped his bat— back and forth, back and forth. He worked the count to three balls and one strike and then he watched a change-up pitch float up to the plate. He let the ball come to him. Then, he snapped his wrists and hit it hard. Home run. Three-run homer for the bonus kid.

"I learned my lesson," Bobby told his pals at dinner that night. "Now, it is all up to me. I know I can hit. You saw it today and yesterday. I saw it, too.

Nobody has to trick me any more, or lead me by the hand. I know I can do it on my own."

Bobby swept the last carrots into his mouth and cut into his steak. He looked around the apartment and grinned. "I never thought I would be having dinner with you guys tonight."

All week, Bobby's booming home runs brought him stories in the papers. Against the Eagles, he stepped into a fast ball and belted it over the 460-foot sign and clear across the street. A parking lot attendant complained to the Sox the next day that the ball had cracked the glass in a car window.

"Cracked a car window," Speed Peters yelled. "That lot is at least 150 feet from the fence. How about that! The ball goes 610 feet!"

The Sox went on the road for a two-week trip and fans filled the ball parks in every city to see the bonus kid. They rooted for him everywhere. In Chicago, Leo Gallagher kicked up clouds of dust in the Bears' third base coaching box. "Listen to them cheer for Reynolds," Leo said. "You would think we were playing in Cleveland. Some home team fans!"

"Leo, my boy," Louie Ziller said. "That's the way the baseball ricochets."

Louie grinned. "You like that? I learned that one from Roger Saltin. Ricochet. Rebound. That's a 64-dollar word."

"No, I don't like it," Leo said.

Louie covered his grin with his glove.

Tony and Charlie came in for a full share of praise, too. The papers began calling them "The Keystone Whiz Kids."

"Those two guys are each 22 years old," Yank told the newspaper men. "And they are making plays as though they had been in the big league for ten years. Reynolds in only 18 and he's hitting like an old pro, too. I got the three best rookies in baseball—Luco, Lewis and Reynolds."

Bobby, Tony and Charlie celebrated wherever they went. They ate in the best restaurants. Don, The Beachcomber's in Chicago, Twenty-One in New York, Loch Ober in Boston. Wherever they went, people knew them and they were mobbed.

Men and women surrounded their tables to ask them to sign their names. "Please, for my little boy," they always said.

On a day off in New York, the rookies planned to go to the theater. "Let's see *Flight to the Clouds*," Charlie said. "I hear it is great."

"Supposed to be," Bobby said. "I read the review in the New York *Times* when the show opened."

"The New York *Times*?" Tony said. "How did you get the *Times* in Waring, Indiana?"

"We have the Sunday *Times* mailed to us every week," Bobby said. "My Pop has made me read it since I began high school. Now it's become a habit."

"We can talk about newspapers later," Charlie said. "Let's get the theater tickets now."

Bobby walked up to the booth in the hotel where theater tickets were sold. He leaned on the counter and spoke softly to the fellow who waited on him.

"I would like three tickets for *Flight to the Clouds*," Bobby said. "For tonight."

The fellow behind the counter threw up his hands and laughed. "You would, huh?" he said. "So would one million other people in this town."

Bobby smiled. "I didn't know. Sold out, huh?"

"Biggest since *My Fair Lady*. Say, aren't you Bobby Reynolds of the Sox?"

"Yes."

"Just wait one second. Let me get the boss."

The fellow disappeared through a glass door and came back a minute later with a short man dressed in a shiny silk suit.

"Bobby Reynolds," the short man said. "Well, I'll be darned." The man stuck out his hand. "I'm Sam Poland," he said. "Glad to meet you. That was some home run you hit yesterday."

"Thank you, sir," Bobby said.

The man pulled a sheet of paper from beneath the counter. "Sign this, will you please? Make it to Lenny, my son."

Bobby signed the paper.

"You want tickets to *Flight to the Clouds,* huh?"
Bobby nodded.

"Biggest hit in town," the man said.

"So I hear, sir."

"Well, I just happen to have three seats. Saving
them for one of my big customers." The short man
reached beneath the counter and came up with a
small envelope. "Take them. No charge. Hit a home
run for me tomorrow."

Bobby blushed. "Thank you, sir, but I would like
to pay for them."

"Pay for them? Nothing doing. When Sam Poland gives you a present, he gives you a present. Wait
until I tell the boys at the club that I met Bobby

Reynolds today. That will give them a thrill."

Bobby was famous. He appeared on television shows in every city. In Boston, he was put on Pete Dugan's show right after the ball game. Bobby stood there, sweat running down his face, as Dugan introduced him.

"We have the Golden Boy with us today," Dugan said. "Bobby Reynolds, the Golden Boy. He just won today's game with a 500-foot homer. A Sox victory all because of Bobby Reynolds."

Bobby smiled into the camera. "Thank you, Pete," he said, "but I'm not winning games alone. Nobody can do that. We couldn't have won today if Phil Robinson hadn't pitched a beautiful game. He threw a three-hitter, remember that. And I could not have hit that home run if Red Castigan hadn't singled before I got up. If Red hadn't made that hit, it would have been three out and we would have lost the game. And you can't forget that great catch Barry Regan made in the sixth inning. He saved a sure two runs."

Bobby walked to his locker with bouncy steps. "I should have done that from the beginning," he thought. "That was my big mistake. Don't take all the credit. Just accept it and give credit to everybody else who deserves it. What a dope I was! That was so easy today, and it was the right thing to do. That is what Sage Hawkins meant when he told me to remember there are other guys in the ball club. I should have been doing that from the beginning."

"All of a sudden I have found myself," he wrote to his dad. "I am hitting the ball and I know I am going to keep on hitting the ball. We are having a great time, Tony and Charlie and I. Lard, Roger and Louie are my friends, too. But the other guys still don't like to talk to me. I guess they are afraid of getting Tenda mad at them. Sometimes, even now, I get the feeling I don't really belong."

chapter 12

BEAT THE BENGALS!

Every seat at Sox Park was filled. Horns were blowing, drums were booming. The Bengals were in town.

Bobby ran out of the dugout and stopped short. "Look at that crowd," he yelled. "You couldn't get another guy in here with a shoehorn."

"Just like the World Series," Lard said.

Big, bright signs hung from the railing. BEAT THE BENGALS, the signs read. BEAT THE BENGALS AND WIN THE PENNANT.

At any time, a Bengal-Sox game filled the park, but this one was something special. It was still early in the season, but already the pennant seemed to depend on the games between the Bengals and the

Sox. The two teams were tied now for first place. They were moving far ahead of everybody else, and this was a welcome-home game. The Sox had been away for two weeks during which the fans had had time to miss them. They were eager to see the Keystone Whiz Kids and they were eager to see Bobby Reynolds. The Golden Boy had been belting home runs in every stadium on the road and the fans wanted to see if he could hit them in Sox Park, too.

Tenda stood at the edge of the dugout, glaring at the Bengals. He buckled on his catcher's gear and ran toward home plate. "Get them, gang," he yelled.

The Sox ran out behind the big catcher and the stands exploded with cheers.

"Come on, Sox."

"Beat the Bengals. Beat the Bengals."

"Come on, big Tom. Come on, Bobby."

Roger Saltin flipped his warm-up pitches into Tenda's big mitt. Bobby stood in rightfield, tugging at his cap. He felt the butterflies in his stomach. "What a crowd," he thought. "What a great big crowd! I bet even Tenda feels nervous."

Tony and Charlie stood talking near second base. Tony scraped up dirt with his toe. Charlie pounded his glove.

"Big game," Tony said.

"Biggest I ever played in," Charlie said.

Lard Jennings kicked at the gate out in the Sox

bull pen. Lard had been in the thick of many pennant battles, but he still felt nervous during important games. "You have to feel those butterflies," he said to Gordon. "I don't care how many big games you have played in, you have to feel those butterflies."

The sun beat down on Barry Regan's head. He sprayed tobacco juice into the grass. "If we win this one, we get the big jump," he thought. "Roger, pitch like you never pitched before."

Tenda flipped the baseball to the mound and took his place behind the plate. The Bengals' first batter stepped in. Saltin fired a fast ball for a strike.

"Way to pitch, Roger. Way to pitch," Louie called to him.

The fans howled. "All the way, all the way, all the way."

"If they yell like that for a strike," Bobby thought, "they are likely to tear the place down if we score a run."

Runs were easier to think about than to score. For five innings, neither team even moved a runner to third base. Saltin was pitching a neat game. So was Lester Watt.

In the top of the sixth, Wally Rhino caught hold of one of Saltin's curve balls. Wally was a big man, six feet three inches and 210 pounds, and he put every ounce of energy behind his big swing. He smashed the baseball against the rightfield fence and it bounced back with such force that Charlie, running out from second base was the first man to reach it. He wheeled to throw, but the runner already was standing on second with a double.

Jimmy Gerber sliced Saltin's next pitch to centerfield. It was a clean single and Rhino barreled home with the first run of the game.

"We can get it back," the fans shouted.

"Keep pitching, Roger. Keep throwing hard. One run is nothing."

The one run may have seemed like nothing, but it looked larger as the ball game went on. After eight innings, the Sox still had not scored and in the top of the ninth, the Bengals seemed about to break the game wide open. They loaded the bases with one out, and Tim Abernathy, the big catcher, was coming up to bat. O'Connor walked slowly from the dugout to speak with Saltin.

The buzz in the stands faded as Yank approached Roger. The pitcher and the manager stood together, talking quietly. Tenda, his mask in his hand, joined them.

"My arm seems to be getting tight," Roger said. He swung it around his head. "It hurts when I throw hard. Just a little pain, though. I can keep firing. I don't mind it."

Yank stared toward the bull pen. His wrinkled face was hard with thought. "No," he said. "You have

gone far enough." He gave the sign that meant a
new pitcher was to come in from the bull pen.

The roar that followed from the stands was meant
for two men, Saltin, who was leaving the game, and
Lard Jennings, who was walking slowly in to take his
place.

"Please, Lard," Bobby said to himself, "get us out
of this. Get us out of this. Make him hit it to me.
I'll throw the guy out at the plate. Make him hit it
to me."

Lard tugged his cap and hitched up his pants. He
pounded his glove and he smoothed the dirt on the
mound. The old pro had learned through the years
to take his time in tough spots.

Lard seemed to be counting every stitch on the baseball. "Throw it," Louie yelled. "Throw it hard."

Lard tugged his cap once more. Then he swung into his wind-up. His right arm flashed forward with a knuckle ball. Abernathy whipped his bat. The ball shot back at Lard as if it had been fired from a cannon. It kicked wildly off his knee.

Tony tore in from shortstop and scooped up the ball with his bare hand. He could have thrown home for a sure force-out, but he had other ideas. Tony wanted the double play. He wanted to take the big chance and get the Sox out of trouble. He fired the ball as he fell and it reached second base at the same instant that Charlie cut across the bag.

Rhino's hard slide dumped Charlie to the ground, but the ball was gone from his hands. Charlie had thrown it as soon as it had hit his glove. He fell in a heap with Rhino and watched Red Castigan pluck the ball out of the air at first base. Abernathy crashed into Red, but Red held onto the ball.

"Did you see that! Did you ever see anything like that!"

"What a play. What a great play."

"That Luco is wonderful. So is that Lewis. What a double play!"

The fans pounded each other on the back. They were yelling and jumping in the stands. The Sox still had a chance.

Tenda walked to the plate, squeezing the handle of his bat.

"Come on, big Tom," Louie called. "Come on, boy."

Tom stepped into the box and glared at Watt. The pitcher stared back and wound up. The ball came in fast and chest high. Tenda hit it on the ground, between the shortstop and the third baseman. It was a clean single.

Red Castigan stood up in the on-deck circle, then walked to the dugout for instructions.

"Lay down a bunt," Yank said. "Get Tom to second."

Castigan tried to bunt the first pitch. He nicked the ball with the top of his bat. It was a short pop-up. Abernathy raced in front of the plate and gobbled up the baseball. One out, and Tom was still on first.

Bobby Reynolds thought the fans were going to rip the park apart. Their roars rolled across the field in a roll of thunder as he walked up to the plate. They begged him to get a hit. They yelled at him. They clapped until their hands were red.

"Our last inning," Yank yelled. "Our last inning."

Tony stood at the top of the dugout steps whistling. Charlie banged his glove against the water fountain. Barry Regan crowded in next to Tony and colored the ground with tobacco juice. "Come on, kid!" Barry shouted. "Come on!"

Bobby planted his feet in the batter's box and he pumped his bat back and forth. He let the first pitch go by. It was a strike.

Bobby swung at the second pitch and missed. Abernathy held out the baseball. "That is a curve ball, kid," he said. "Haven't you learned to hit them yet?"

"I hit them," Bobby snapped. "Don't worry."

Abernathy ran to the mound. "Remember the pitch you got him with last time? The waste pitch?"

Watt nodded.

"Get him again," Abernathy said. "Now."

Abernathy walked back behind the plate. Watt wound up and threw the ball wide of the strike zone. "He is trying to get me with the waste pitch," Bobby thought. "Not this time." The bat stayed on Bobby's shoulders. The count became one ball and two strikes.

The next pitch curved toward the outside corner. "This is it," Bobby said to himself. He let go a smooth, level swing and hit the ball into the right-centerfield corner. It climbed higher and higher, faster and faster.

"It is going out of the park, out of the park," Yank began to shout.

The ball flew toward the fence, high enough to clear it. Suddenly, it hooked and crashed into the clock, which towered ten feet above the fence.

"What luck," Charlie groaned. "What luck. He

can't get beyond third base no matter what he does."

Tenda had been off with the crack of the bat. By the time the ball hit the clock, Tom was digging his spikes into second base and turning. Bobby was around first, his arms pumping, his feet kicking up dust.

The ball caught for a second in the clock tower, then fell slowly to the ground. The Bengal center-fielder stood waiting for it, begging for the ball to hurry into his glove. When it finally did, he turned to throw.

Tenda was digging for the plate, Bobby was rushing toward third and Billy Templeton was waving him home. "Go all the way," Billy yelled. "Go all the way." Billy's arm was circling the air like a cowboy swinging a lasso.

The centerfielder fired the ball toward home. It was a good throw. It reached the plate on the second bounce. Abernathy grabbed it and braced himself, blocking the base.

"He has the ball," the fans yelled. "Bobby is going to be out at home."

Bobby had two choices. He could slide in and hope to hook around Abernathy, or he could come in standing and try to knock the ball out of the big catcher's mitt. Bobby rushed in standing up. He smashed into the catcher and knocked him over.

Abernathy tumbled back and the ball flew from

his glove. Bobby stepped on home plate and ran happily to the dugout.

The fans roared for a full five minutes, but Bobby only heard the first earth-shaking shout. The Sox almost carried him into the club house. Tony whistled. Charlie yelled. Yank O'Connor pounded him on the back. Lard Jennings shook his hand so hard that Bobby thought it would come off. When he reached his locker, it was surrounded by writers.

The writers wanted to know everything. When did he decide to try for home? Why did he come in standing up, instead of sliding? Did he see Abernathy try to push through the crowd after him?

"I decided to try for home only when Templeton

waved me in. I came in standing up because the catcher had the plate blocked. I didn't see Abernathy come after me. You sure he did?"

More questions. More answers. The sweat poured down Bobby's smiling face. The writers would not leave him alone. Finally, he peeled off his drenched uniform and headed for the showers. Charlie and Tony were already dressed.

"Meet you back at the apartment," Charlie said. "We want to get some great big steaks on the fire. We are serving you tonight, you big hero."

Bobby slapped Charlie's arm and mussed up Tony's hair. "See you later," he said.

By the time Bobby was dressed, most of the Sox were gone. He walked alone through the halls to the exit. It was dim under the stands. A strong arm reached out and held him. It was Tim Abernathy's arm. And Wally Rhino was standing beside him.

"You play pretty rough," Abernathy said.

"You play pretty rough for a rookie," Rhino added.

"Get out of my way," Bobby said.

"Why don't you knock us out of your way?" Rhino said. "Like you did Tim in the ball game."

"That was in the ball game," Bobby said. "You play hard in the ball game."

"Not unless you can back it up," Abernathy said.

"I don't want to fight," Bobby said.

"Why not?" Rhino said. "You are a big boy."

"It is a long story," Bobby said.

"Forget your story," Abernathy said. "You are going to fight, whether you like it or not. If you play rough in the ball game, you be ready to back it up with your fists."

Bobby stared straight ahead. He slid his ring up and down his finger. "I can take either one of them," he thought. "I don't want to, but I can."

"What are you thinking about, rookie?" Rhino demanded.

"Which one of you do I have to fight?" Bobby said.

The two Bengals laughed. "Which one of us?" Abernathy said. "Why, both of us, rookie."

Both of them! Bobby had not even thought of that. He couldn't take on two such big men at one time.

"We are going to teach you a lesson, rookie," Rhino said. "You ready to learn, rookie?"

"Both of us are ready to learn. Who is going to teach us?"

It was Tom Tenda. He had been there all the time, hidden in the shadows. Now he was out in the open, standing beside Bobby.

"Come on," Tenda said. "Teach us a lesson." He barked his words and doubled up his fists. "Teach us a lesson. Come on. Start teaching."

Abernathy looked at Rhino. Rhino looked at Bobby and Tenda. The Bengals wheeled around toward the exit. "We will get you in the ball game tomorrow," Rhino called over his shoulder.

"Any time," Tenda said. "In the ball game."

Bobby turned to the catcher. "Thank you, Tom," he said. "Thank you."

Tenda grinned and put his arm around Bobby's shoulder. "That's okay, kid," he said. "Us Sox have to stick together."